ONE MURDER TOO MANY

Wayne Clark

Published by Wayne Clark YUL/NYC

ISBN: 978-1-7751915-9-9

Cover and book design: Nell Chitty

Cover image: Jerome Robbins Dance Division,
The New York Public Library for the Performing Arts

ACKNOWLEDGEMENTS

The author would like to thank Julia Clark-Combot
for her encouragement and insightful editing assistance
and for her service as uncompromising critic.

CONTENTS

CHAPTER 1

"TELL me again about how you met Mom?" The young woman sat at the end of the cigarette-scarred wooden table in what the man called his dining room. She would laugh, too, every time he called it that. In reality, it was the only table in the only room in his apartment. It sat at the foot of his bed. The kitchen was so tiny it could hardly be called a room. The restroom was down the hall, shared with the building's seven other tenants.

Every time Eve asked the question—and she did at least once a year—she looked straight into the man's eyes. They were gentle as always. They betrayed his bulk, a physique that once stretched his police patrolman's uniform to the ripping point. His forehead, she always thought, protruded a little too much, but the eyes made up for that. Besides, he had more words than she ever would. There were no books in the flat so she didn't know where he got his vocabulary.

She often reminded herself that it was probably strange to keep looking at his face and body, her a young woman and him an older man, but she couldn't help it. It wasn't sexual. For some reason since her mother's death it had become important to know how her mother saw him. He'd been her hero. She told Eve that more than once. Now that she was grown up, she realized that Humph had become a paternal figure for her. Sometimes his mere size made her feel like a little kid again and his gentle eyes made her feel somehow that no matter what was going on in her life he'd always be there for her. She often cursed herself for not visiting more often.

His body was a contradiction of sorts, she thought. It didn't belong to his nature. Like a piece of pork packed in a can meant for corn kernels, or something like that.

His name was Humph, Humphrey Barstal. In his former life, as a cop, his precinct knew him as Officer Barstool. He drank a lot in those days. They all did. Now he was a private eye. He still drank a lot but for different reasons. When he drank now, he'd be on a boredom binge. He rarely got cases, at least paying ones. When he was a cop, he drank every day out of disgust with himself for holding that job. The idea of being a cop sounded good in the beginning but the day-to-day slog destroyed that notion. The boys were okay to work with, most of them at least, but they were for the most part grade-school dropouts trying to game the system that paid them small potatoes. Small potatoes weren't enough for an Irishman, which most of them were.

Most of the hoodlums they tried to chase down were their Irish brethren as well. That's just the way it was downtown. It was like they were fighting their own civil war just to put some whiskey on the table.

Sunny Frances, Eve's mom, had been Humph's great love. Ever since he came into their lives, Eve knew that. Despite all his words, which she learned about later, he never said a lot to her mom. But he never took his eyes off her. He was devoted to her to the tips of her toes. Her mom always said the job would kill him. Instead, she was the one who ended up dead.

Humph rarely mentioned her death but he was always happy to talk about meeting Sunny. He said that, in a way, she was the real reason he got booted off the force.

It was now seven years since Humph and Eve suddenly found themselves alone. She was christened Evelyn but as a toddler she never responded to her full name or perhaps she was already testing the rebellious side of her nature. She was an "Eve" from the get-go, her mom told Humph. Eve was now only 22 and Humph figured the pain he felt was probably a hundred times less than what Eve felt. Eve had been only 15 when her mom died. The family next door took her in.

When Humph set out to answer Eve's question about what their first meeting was like, it made Sunny alive again and it made Humph relive the most glorious feeling life had ever bestowed on him. He didn't grow up thinking life offered all that much to anyone, so maybe he'd already tasted the sweetest moments.

They met on a chilly night in November 1921. Humph and another constable were on what they laughingly called Protection Patrol, or PP duty. Their assignment for the night was to walk specific streets where prostitutes were known to parade themselves. That night, they were primarily strolling 30th and 29th Streets, just east of Broadway. They knew most of the girls. They'd nod to each other, or even stop and chat before moving on. The girls knew not to sass them too much. The cops could, and often did what they wanted with them.

If they worked out of bordellos, the bordellos themselves paid the cops monthly and if the cops thought that the bordellos were doing especially good business, sometimes weekly. In those cases, that money went straight up the police ladder to the muckety-mucks. As for the girls, paying protection money meant they wouldn't be hassled on their assigned streets but what the cops were really hoping to see was one of them venture onto a street that hadn't been assigned to them. If one of these girls turned up to 31st Street, for example, Bingo!, as Humph's partner used to say. The cops imposed a $5 fine, which was negotiable, payable on the spot, or it was off to the hoosegow for them and an appearance before the magistrate for prostitution.

A portion of that money had to go to their sergeant. He was good at counting. If the evening's take was too little, he'd accuse the boys of either holding back on him or sluffing off.

"What happened? You spent the night whoring?"

They'd have to pay out of their own pockets the amount the sarge thought he was owed. Loan sharks were more understanding.

On that night in November, on East 32nd Street, a woman wearing an elegant black coat that reached her ankles stopped at a red light.

"Too much of a looker for this neighborhood," ruled Humph's partner in his judge and jury voice. Nevertheless, the two cops jaywalked to the intersection to wait for the young lady to cross.

She made the mistake of saying, "Evening, boys."

Humph's partner, Eugene Evans, pounced.

"Sorry, honey, but you're out of bounds. This here is 32nd Street in case you hadn't noticed."

"So?" she replied, staring right back at him, and not at all intimidated.

Without hesitating, Eugene, a man with a wife who was afraid of mice, grabbed the brunette's arm and started to turn her west toward Broadway. He took one step in that direction and his other knee buckled all the way to the pavement. Eugene later admitted, while showing the bruise, that the kick had landed like the blade of a knife directly below his kneecap.

"Must be a fuckin' steel-tipped shoe or something," he protested when boys at the precinct later grilled him for information about the dame who dropped him in his tracks.

With his partner incapacitated and spluttering a role-call of obscenities, it had fallen to Humph to escort the lady back to the precinct.

"Ma'am," he said. "Just come with me. It won't take too long, I reckon."

"I suppose I'll be charged with assault?" she asked. Humph liked the fact that it was a matter-of-fact question, not a haughty how-dare-you challenge. This girl had been around, he guessed.

With Eugene hobbling behind, exclaiming that, "That broad is gonna pay big time. Mark my fucking words, Humph!", Humph couldn't hold his smirk any longer. His prisoner saw it. Her eyes betrayed a smile.

At the station, Eugene, gasping, latched onto the top of the sergeant's big desk, still bleating. Humph still held the prisoner's arm. To her, it felt as if he were escorting her to a restaurant or a club. His big mitt held her forearm and she knew there was no escape but there was no pressure in his grip. Exhausted by the nonsense, she leaned lightly against his frame.

"Are you finished?" the sergeant asked Eugene.

"I guess I am, sir."

"So," the sergeant said, "you want me to write up the charge as assaulting a police officer, causing bodily harm?"

"Yes sir. Exactly what she did. Wanna see my knee?"

"Eugene, lad. Go get pissed somewhere. Get pissed out of your skull and await delivery of your medal for bravery."

"Humph, what do you got to say?"

"The lady's not a whore."

"And you know that how?"

"During our long walk back to the station, she expressed concern for the bawling uniform we had in tow, by that I mean Officer Evans. Furthermore, though she had plenty of opportunity, she never uttered a sweet nothin' in my ear. Were she a lady of the night, she would assuredly have done so in hope of escaping justice. And finally, Officer Evans and I know every single one of the girls on the stroll in this neighborhood. This lady isn't one of them. I kinda wish she were. A little gratitude from someone like her would make a man's day, I swear."

"Take her home with our apologies, Humph."

"And that's how we met," Humph said to Eve. "I took her home, she made tea, and you know the rest."

The rest wasn't instant. Sunny was too good for him, he feared. It wasn't just the elegant black coat she wore the night he steered her away from magistrate's court. There was something else. She had the confidence to keep her own counsel. Although she was indeed grateful for her rescue, it was only on the third meeting for tea that she told Humph how she supported herself.

She had grown up in vaudeville.

"The singing and dancing and the silly skits, that's me," Sunny said with a smile. "That's the whole story, except that my game is burlesque now. I'm my own act. I like it that way."

"What's the difference between vaudeville and burlesque?" Humph asked.

Sunny laughed. "I've heard it said the burlesque is vaudeville's horny sister. Let's say we're more titillating than your run-of-the-mill vaudeville production."

Over the next few meetings, Humph realized that show business was her whole life, not just her meal ticket. She was happy when she talked about it. She said that one of the things she enjoyed most about it was working with women who do what they want and don't sit around waiting for a man's approval.

Humph had no idea what she was talking about except that he knew that life had changed a lot, especially for women, since the end of the Great War.

As a cop, he had cleared the streets for women marching for the vote, which he guessed was alright, and women marching against booze, which wasn't alright.

He'd been to burlesque theaters but most of those times had been in the role of a cop conducting a raid. None of the other cops seemed to really know why they were told to go on these raids. They never found any real criminals and rarely even a pickpocket stupid enough to keep lifting wallets after the cops burst in. Sometimes there was a story in the papers the next day, quoting some self-important guy in a suffocating suit who said things like, "Salvation resides on the moral high road." He praised the lads in blue for being on the front line of the war for decency in New York. Even Humph's sergeant shrugged when asked what the politician was yammering on about.

Nevertheless, what he glimpsed during those raids, and the sounds he heard as he and the other cops assembled on the street outside the theater, did nothing to dampen his interest in seeing for himself what Sunny so enthusiastically described. He knew which theater she worked at and, without telling her his intentions, he twice bought a ticket and sat far from the stage.

When he eventually told Sunny that he'd twice seen her perform, she admonished him for hiding in the back.

"When I'm on stage, I don't have to be proper. I'd have enjoyed dedicating my eyes to the giant in the audience as I danced and, well, you know."

Humph knew her well by then and Sunny's comment didn't make him blush as it would have in the past. He wasn't a prude but men and women simply didn't cross certain lines.

CHAPTER 2

HUMPH didn't have to wait another year before seeing Eve. A week after their last visit together, she was at the door again.

"Forgot my stole," she said. "And by the way, here's a copy of the latest *True Manhattan Detective.*

"How could you forget something like that? It's luxury. Nothing less. Makes a lady out of you, girl, not that you are anything less than a lady, I mean."

"Humph, it's not real fur. I'm not in that league." After a moment of enjoying his embarrassment, Eve added:

"Yet."

Humph ushered her in and pointed to the chair at the familiar table. He stuck his head in his closet and returned with the stole.

"Mink? Yes?"

"Fake mink," Eve said with a laugh.

"Well, I'd settle for fake any day," Humph replied. "Never knew a girl with a stole."

"Can I get you something?" Humph offered.

"I know you're always trying to enact your very own personal Prohibition, but I can't believe you don't still indulge once in a while."

"Well, I guess that's true enough," said Humph. "A gent has gotta exercise his elbow once in a while."

"In that case, would you mind if I asked for a glass? I have a flask in my purse. The nights are getting cold."

Humph found a glass. He wouldn't have done it for himself but for Eve a good wipe with a towel, inside and out, was called for.

"You're not working the streets again, are you?"

Eve could see he was legitimately concerned. She didn't reply. After two gulps of her vodka, she nodded yes.

She watched Humph's face, focusing on the small eyes buried in his big smart head. There was no judgment. Humph had been around. In fact he'd probably seen more of mankind's nature than she would ever know.

"Yeah, my last show closed and all the others seem to be set for a while. No casting calls that I know of. Stripped for a while on Bowery but the money was shit and the guys shittier. Not like the Village."

Humph had long ago noted that Eve swore like many young women these days. Her mom would have been shocked.

"Rent up to date?" Humph asked.

It was a typical Humph reaction. Practical, realistic. To a fault. They'd had a conversation like this before. Even though he'd once been a flatfoot, he didn't necessarily hate the bad guys. Maybe that's why Humph stopped being a cop. He knew too well that the bad guys were like him. They tripped up while trying to figure out how to live this life, just like anybody else. Well-off people tripped up, too, but they always had something soft to fall on.

Part of Eve wanted to go to the other side of the table and plunk herself down on the big lunk's lap, just to plant a kiss on his cheek as a silent thank you for not judging. If it hadn't been her mom that he'd loved, she would have done so. Humph was still the only real dad she'd known.

"Yes. Rent up to date and there's enough under my mattress for next month."

"Mattress? That's stupid, Eve. That's the first place anyone looks."

Eve was taken aback. He was scolding her, seriously. Then she looked at his face again. It was a father's concern.

"From now on, leave your money with me," he said. It was an order. She'd never seen him so dominant.

"Of course. Yeah. Why didn't I think of that?"

They talked for about an hour, entirely about her. Humph made it like that. He rarely talked about himself.

Finally, Eve said:

"Talk to me! What in heaven's name are you doing these days? Are you alive? Are you half-dead? Do you have friends?"

Humph lowered his little eyes for the first time since she'd arrived.

"I'm reasonably certain I'm alive because I still cry inside for your momma." Was it the effects of the belt he'd taken from her flask that helped that admission slip out? No, Eve decided. As Humph said that he was staring hard into Eve's eyes. She knew he was telling the truth.

"In the outside world, I'm surviving. Believe it or not, I've got a case."

Eve knew that even though Humph described himself as a private eye since leaving the police force, he rarely caught a case.

At Eve's continuing insistence, he explained.

"A writer, the son of a rich guy, a real rich guy. He says he's been the victim of a $10,000 stock market scam. He wants to nail the broker who suckered him in. Only problem is, I don't know anything about stocks. As far as I know, brokers are people who are broke."

Eve couldn't help laughing.

"Maybe I can help you, Humph."

She said a guy she'd serviced several times in the past six months was a broker of some kind.

"Me too, I don't understand anything about stocks. But he loves saying how a smart trader has to know how to deceive people. Maybe he can help you."

"Why would he talk to me if he's doing illegal stuff?"

"Because I know his address, I know his wife's name. I could blackmail his pompous ass any time I want."

"Set it up, Sunny. Just tell him I'm a yokel wanting to know why everyone is getting rich on the stock market except himself. Something like that. Don't want to scare him off."

· · ·

The arrogant young man who wanted to hire Humph was getting impatient. He got on Humph's bad side at their first meeting a month ago. Today, he started their phone conversation with a threat:

"You'd better have news, PI guy."

Humph wasn't the type to get flustered but he also never hesitated to stand his ground. He dug back at his client.

"I need to study up more on the stock market. What puzzles me is how a smart guy like you with all your money and your Fordham education got suckered for $10 grand. That's something I might expect from a dumb guy."

His client hung up.

Half an hour later, he phoned back.

"Sorry, Humphrey. I suddenly remembered I had to see a man about a dog. Holding a party tonight."

"First of all, I don't answer to Humphrey. Secondly, don't drink the jake you just bought for your party. I want to talk to you face to face and I'd prefer it if you're sober."

"After the petting party, my place is going to be a shambles next Monday," said the young man. "We'll meet at my parent's place, on Bainbridge Avenue in the Bronx. Let's say 11 a.m."

Humph couldn't place the street. He imagined there must be some ritzy places around there. Monday worked for him as well. It would give him time to lose his resentment of the man who hopefully would end up paying handsomely if the case were solved.

Humph had already decided to wait as long as possible before telling the kid that people got scammed all the time and there was almost never anything that could be done about it. You have to catch someone with his hand in your pocket or forget about it. This way, Humph figured, he could build up some billable hours before the client baled.

The next morning, Humph called the kid before leaving to confirm the time and the address.

"Humph? Humph who?" was the initial response at the other end of the line. "Oh, oh yeah. Sorry. I got good and zozzled last night. Can we put this on hold for a day or two?"

Ordinarily, Humph would have dug up some more synonyms for dumb but he was happy to wait. He was waiting for Eve to say she'd hogtied a broker for him. Humph really needed to pick his brains to understand how brokers picked investors' pockets.

Two days later, Eve came through. She'd hog-tied her broker and, putting him under the threat of blackmail, was overjoyed to pass him on to Humph.

Humph did a lot of asking around on Wall Street, the pop-up brokerages that wanted to profit from the public's new wide-eyed aspirations and downright greed. Some brokers even printed their own front pages, pretending that the *Mirror* or the *Daily News* had proclaimed in two-inch-high letters that American stocks were the new El Dorado. "Good as gold," claimed one headline. No need to sail the seven seas anymore to find the lost city of gold. Board a tram and get off at Wall Street.

"Welcome America!" cried one poster in front of a skinny two-story building that was once a barrel-making establishment. Humph remembered the place from his rookie days as a flatfoot. The proprietor was friendly enough. If memory served, he was an Idaho-born potato farmer. The only barrel Humph ever saw there was stamped with the name Samuel Bronfman, the whiskey man.

It piqued his curiosity but it wasn't something he could take to his precinct's detectives. In Yiddish, the surname meant "liquor man." Humph's first seven years on this planet were spent with a Jewish family on the Lower East Side. Before he even went to school, they had taught him to read and write. They also taught him Yiddish. The couple thought Humph had potential, even in the suffocating world of Lower East Side immigrants. They were deprived of the chance of seeing their hopes come true one night in 1917 when Humph was arrested for vagrancy.

The charge, even to a teenager's mind, was preposterous. He pleaded that he was looking for scraps of food near restaurants. His family needed food, and they needed him, he said. The cops asked where he supposedly lived. He said, "On Hester Street." The cop replied, "So do a couple of thousand other invaders. Give me the exact address." Apparently, thought Humph, the cop didn't like immigrants.

When Humph said he didn't know the number, the cop said he was under arrest. The reason Humph didn't know the street number was that long before he had been taken in by the family someone had posted a sign over the number. It read: "Jesus Saves". Humph never knew who this guy Jesus was or whether he really lived in the building.

After his arrest, Humph was shuffled off to a foster home. It was run by some outfit known as Orphan Train. Much later, he learned their objective was to move as many orphans out of New York City as possible. They didn't nab them all. He was one of the kids who got to stay in the city.

When Humph was 17, he ran away and learned he had two options. Join the army to fight in the European war or join the New York Police Department. He chose the latter and soon rejoiced in his decision. There was no real training offered. They wanted bodies to patrol the streets. The pay was pitiful but he got a uniform and respect, or so he thought at first. Later he learned that his massive frame and his fists were the only things that earned respect on downtown New York streets.

When Humph arrived at the broker's office, he realized the guy might be obscenely successful but he was smart enough to keep a low profile.

His address was the same as the one Humph encountered as a rookie cop. It was the old barrel maker's, the one that was probably an importer of Canadian booze. The building was utterly nondescript, apart from a bronze, or bronze-imitation company name plate to the right of the entrance, and inside, a bronze-and-black floor indicator above the elevator. Those bronze touches were new.

The building was only three stories tall so Humph wondered why anyone had forked out money for a fancy elevator. Maybe, he thought, it was a cultural thing, have-nots vs haves.

On the slow ride up the elevator, and, based on what Eve told him about this broker guy, Humph decided to play dumber than he looked. Perhaps the approach would be an invitation to the guy's greedy ego to slather it on. Humph hoped the guy would get carried away with himself and betray a common con that a broker might have played on the rich kid.

The broker's name was Ostenbruch. Eve said it was pronounced "Osten Brook", like a fishing stream in the Adirondacks.

The problem, as Humph saw it, was the same as any court would see it. Sweet talking somebody into risking their money was no crime. The onus is on the dodo.

He would have to catch the broker in some kind of lie. Since Eve's slave was immensely successful, there was little chance he'd be dumb enough to admit chicanery.

This, Humph decided, would be little more than a fact-finding mission, an investment—an appropriate term, he thought—in a future collar.

The broker greeted him warmly, having been primed by a threatening Eve.

He babbled on for almost 20 minutes.

While he did so, Humph sat in a hard wooden chair. He wished it swiveled to give his joints a break. As he lectured about himself, the broker slowly paced around his office. Behind Humph, then around his desk, then in front of the desk with his thumbs in his waistcoat pockets. Why did short cigar-smokers always do that? How many of them, Humph wondered as the broker's face broke into a condescending smile, know how to spell the word *magniloquent*? Humph had never uttered the word in his life but he'd read it and it just popped into his head as he stared at the broker.

"Mr. Humphrey, I see you're not taking notes. I was led to believe you wanted the real inside deal on how street brokers work."

Humph pretended to ponder his reply although he'd formed his opinion in the first minute.

"Well, sir, you've certainly added to my vocabulary," he said, nodding to himself, as if reflecting on all he'd learned. In reality, he was staring at the floor as he nodded. That gave him time to relish his comeback, which he hoped would put the windbag in his place and lead to some useful information.

"Bucket shops, margins, margin trading, margin loans, marginal investments, equity requirements," Humph said, counting each term on his fingertips. "I can't even recall half the terms you taught me."

The broker beamed and knocked the ash off his cigar, letting it fall to the floor.

"But you haven't told me how you reel in a sucker. Earlier, if I remember correctly, you said suckers are the driving force in your business."

"Well," said the broker, back in his chair with his feet on his desk, "let me put things another way. Do you fish, big fella?"

"No. I'm not a fan of water or what comes out of it. Someone's always fishing a body out of the East River. Bodies in the Hudson probably end up gracing the shores of New Jersey. So, no fishing metaphors please."

The broker chuckled.

"OK, all I was going to say is that we brokers don't have to reel in suckers. They tend to reel themselves in. Their greed is the bait and it plunks them right in our lap. End of fishing meta-whatever you called them.

"You could go to the Grand Canyon and people there would all know that the stock market can make you rich. Instead of breaking your back working all day for a buck fifty, you plunk that buck fifty on the barrel head at a stockbroker's office and he can turn that into a fortune. No labor required. Investing doesn't build calluses on your hands. There are stories in the paper every other day about laborers and the like bathing in undreamed of wealth. Walk into any speakeasy and you'll hear the boasting and see how many new friends the investor has beside him at the bar."

Humph waited for him to continue.

"Where's the catch? And I don't mean the fishing term."

"The catch, sir, is that everyone knows you don't need to have enough money to buy the stocks you've set your heart on. So the poor man sees the stock market as the epitome of democracy. Rich or poor, everyone can play the market."

At that point, the broker hauled his feet off the desktop and leaned forward halfway over his desk. His right index finger leapt into the air as he was about to ram a nail in democracy's coffin.

"Yes sir, the poor guy can plunk down his buck fifty and we dutifully ask if he would like to double his investment. With infinite patience, we explain that if the stock price goes up he might double his money. He and his missus will be able to eat a steak or two for the next few suppers. We then tell him that to double his investment, we will sort of give him money. We mention in passing that that money, the buck fifty we threw in in his name, is a loan. But we add quickly that paying us back will be easy when his investment pays off.

"Believe me, Humph... did I say your name right this time?... the guy's eyes will be so wide he doesn't usually think to ask us straight off about what happens if the stock loses money. By then, he's already reeled himself in. He has bought stock on margin. That's what we call it if you borrow money to make your investment. By not asking what happens if the stock price goes below what we paid, we, the brokerage, he doesn't know that we could sell off the shares. We keep that money, of course, and we charge the rookie investor for the loan amount plus interest. You find yourself poorer than you were before investing.

"At the brokerage, we never lose but you can. I've seen guys lose their shirts then find some shylock who'll lend them some money. They come right back and tell the broker they want to invest again. They know their neighbor went from rags to riches so, by gum as the hicks say, they walk in here convinced that they will, too."

Humph stood up. He needed to stretch his towering six-foot-five-inch frame, he explained to the broker who appeared taken aback at the sudden gesture made while he was in full verbal flight.

Humph did little that wasn't intentional. Now he wanted to turn the sucker lecture to his client's case, the rich kid who got bilked for thousands of dollars. However, he didn't want to make the broker think his business practices were under investigation. He would need to pick his brain down the road, he thought.

"So, I can see how poor people might be easy prey for you…"

"Whoa, we're not vultures, Humph. For heaven's sake."

"That's definitely the impression you give. Anyway, what I want to know is whether you think a college-educated man can be just as much of a sucker as your average Joe."

"We don't get many of those," said Ostenbruch. "Old money tends to deal with the banks. They'll do the investing for them."

The evasive answer told Humph something he had wanted to verify. The kid investor was from old money but he was a defiant young man. The fact that he was an arrogant prick was beside the point. The kid wanted to make it on his own. Humph didn't know yet whether the kid wanted to blow off his overbearing family but he certainly wanted to strike out on his own and confront them as equals. The rich respect rich. The kid would do anything, Humph thought, to be rich. He had no evidence of that but he believed in his instincts.

Had the broker suckered in the kid way beyond his means? Had the broker played on the kid's desire to declare his independence at any cost and become a man of account socially and financially? It looked that way.

The kid was ripe for picking. That's how the broker would have seen him, thought Humph.

Still no crime, he realized, but he now saw how the battle lines were drawn on the brokerage floor.

How had a broker gotten the kid to wager more money than he actually had? He had to talk to the kid. He'd have to lay siege to his arrogance to get at the truth. And, now that he'd been lectured by Eve's conceited slave, Humph felt ready to meet whatever broker the kid had used.

Humph extended his meat-hook hand to Eve's broker in thanks and, while their hands were clasped, said, "The odds, sir, are good that I may want to use your help in the future. I hope you'll be amenable to the idea." The broker, wincing from Humph's grip, mumbled "Of course, sir."

CHAPTER 3

HUMPH was indebted to Eve for setting up the meet with the broker. The guy was far from likable but he was obviously successful and he at least gave Humph a feel for a world that was an open door to broken dreams, deception and possible ruin for the average Joe. But Humph's client was no average Joe. Wealthy, university educated and brimming with the confidence of the select few who have a place reserved for them at birth in New York's social register with the name J. Franklin Norwich. Humph thought of him as simply Frank or Frankie. He did that to make sure he didn't give the kid more credence than he'd give anybody he just met.

As he walked to Chatham Square, at the juncture of Worth Street and the bottom end of the Bowery, Humph felt he was starting out on a school trip. Why he felt that he didn't know. In his seven years in a classroom, he'd never been taken anywhere except the principal's office.

The day was pure gold. Plastered to a deep blue sky, a bold sun stared down at a safe distance from Earth. Any closer and Humph would curse the heat. As he approached the stairs leading up to the Third Avenue El train, Humph's sense of adventure had been tweaked by the fact that he'd never gone so far uptown. The furthest north he'd ever ventured was Yankee Stadium at East 153ʳ Street. He wasn't sure but his destination this morning must be in the 180s or higher. Any further and he'd be in Canada. The thought elicited a shimmering childhood memory of his adoptive Jewish parents talking about relatives in Montreal.

The train made a lot of noise on the tracks. It must have been hell, and sooty, to live under them, Humph thought. But the screeching and clatter added to the adventure somehow. Was he a soldier off to war or just someone who enjoys asking questions of a squirming prisoner? Though Frankie was his client, Humph didn't truly know whether he was a good guy or a bad one. By the return journey, he hoped to have a lot of answers, including details of the brokerage that apparently duped him.

When he finally got off the train and made his way to Bainbridge Avenue, he could have found the house without the street address. It was a two-story stone dwelling on a large lot. It stood out from its neighbors. It had to classify as at least a mini-mansion, Humph figured.

Why rich people made you climb so many stairs to get to the front door he didn't know. The front door at his place on Henry Street in Chinatown had only five.

The butler who answered the door was so short Humph was sure the guy was going to topple over as he titled backwards to take in the tall caller's face.

The guy had a British accent. Does Frankie's dad pay extra to get a British butler, Humph wondered?

"Willy!" The voice was the kid's. "Is the visitor a

Humph-something-or-other?" Frankie was bellowing from the second floor.

"Yes, sir, I do believe it is."

"By the way, sir," the butler said to Humph, "should you care about accuracy, my name is William. Please feel at liberty to call me thusly."

"Of course, William," Humph replied, his voice sympathizing with the butler's burden.

The butler led him into a depressingly Victorian sitting room. The frills and do-dads and the overly busy wallpaper left him dizzy and a touch claustrophobic.

To his surprise, he was relieved when Frankie appeared. He looked like he was about to go out clubbing, or almost. He wore thin-striped, black pants, a white shirt and a bow tie, and black patent shoes. No jacket. Humph deduced he didn't merit full gentlemen's attire.

"Good of you to venture north," Frankie said. "Do you bare good tidings?"

"How could I possibly? You've told me nothing about the incident. People being scammed on Wall Street is hardly unusual. It's a daily fact of modern life. I need every particular you can recall."

Frankie stared at Humph for a moment, obviously discomfited by Humph's directness. On the verge of being impudent, he thought. Frankie took the crease of each leg of his trousers between thumb and index finger and delicately raised his trousers slightly as he sat himself down in an easy chair.

"Willy! Two whiskies!"

He then turned to Humph.

"By the by, I have moved here. This is now my official abode. Pater decided last year that this little home was beneath him. He used mother's passing a few years ago as an excuse to relocate to a true mansion in Greenwich like so many of his social register brothers and sisters. This was my childhood home and I grew to detest the place as

I grew to detest my father. At first, I wanted nothing to do with it. However now that my father has further distanced himself from me—I've never even been to Connecticut and I don't expect an invitation—I find myself quite comfortable here. And I got to keep the butler. Father has hired the butler who has always served at the Connecticut place. The couple who owned it passed away just before my father purchased the place."

"I see," said Humph before getting down to business.

"For starters," Humph said, "I want the name and address of the brokerage, and the name of the broker you dealt with. In all likelihood, I will pay him a visit. Second, I want to know how you heard of this particular brokerage and the names of any acquaintances who perhaps recommended it to you. Or did you wander down Wall Street or Broad and find a building façade that pleased your eye? I see you collect art."

"That's all my mother's. I don't have time to appreciate oily dabs and swirls."

Willy arrived with the drinks. Humph decided to give in to what he regarded as his lower nature and accept the glass. The Scotch might help him win the trust of his cock-sure client.

"Where to start, where to start, old boy." Frankie's butler might well be English but Frankie wasn't. Humph found himself thinking how much he'd enjoy putting this "chappie" in his place. Then his practiced patience regained control.

After Humph reached inside his four-button suit jacket and pulled out a notebook, Frankie furnished the name and address of the broker.

"And the friend or friends who recommended the place….?"

Frankie stared at Humph, then called out to William.

"Willy! Time for a top up. No need to bring a fresh glass."

He waited until the butler replenished both drinks.

Humph said, "Thanks." William inclined his head ever so slightly. Frankie glared at Humph, then explained that Willy was just doing his job. "You don't thank those people for doing what you pay them to do."

Recovered from Humph's faux pas, Frankie continued.

"Odd thing is, while I spoke to several investor friends before taking the leap, the fellow who showed me the light was not much above Willy's station in life. He was a clerk in one of my father's enterprises. I had met him in passing, as it were, during a period when my father was determined to turn me into a businessman in general, and in particular into the man who would one day bestow his behind upon my father's chair at the head of a 60-foot-long marble boardroom table. God's chair to be precise."

Frankie went on to explain that he had no interest in business.

"I want to be a writer."

He then went silent. He stared at Humph. It must have been a full minute before he uttered another word.

"When I confessed my desire to be a writer, you said nothing. Your mouth didn't even twitch. Most mouths in my entourage drop open at the revelation. None of my family would invite a writer to dine with us unless he was a blue blood of some sort."

Humph was grateful for the crystal glass in his left hand. The Scotch gave him an excuse to pause and re-evaluate the kid with knife-edge creases in his trousers. He was one of the few cops in all of New York who kept library books in his locker. He read when sitting around waiting to be called to testify in court, and sometimes even at the start of his shift when the duty sergeant was trying to inspire his soldiers before he sent them out to war on the city's streets. Humph held writers in high esteem. He would love to write. He also knew that a school dropout could never write a book.

Frankie was no drop-out but it now sounded like he

wanted to drop out of high society provided he could keep his butler, his fine bar and his collection of young ladies who specialized in clinging to rich boys like him. Humph had to concede that the kid was fair-to-good looking. Humph also remembered his first conversation with Frankie when it became clear that a weekend-long Bronx bacchanal was of greater concern at that moment than having been ripped off for thousands of dollars by a shady broker.

Frankie finally broke into Humph's thoughts by explaining why this clerk inspired him to invest in the stock market everyone was talking about.

"This damned clerk, who probably didn't even own a dinner jacket, became a millionaire, or close to it, in the time it takes to sail to Southampton and back. He walked into a brokerage named Hodgkins & Co on Broad Street, just south of Wall Street, deposited a paltry sum and watched it turn to gold. He now lives on Park Avenue. I've been there. He has a rather attractive young maid."

Humph had read all the stories about humble Kansas farmers making it big on Wall Street but the stories read like fiction, or a high-powered PR campaign paid for by brokerages.

"I'm going to have to meet him. Can you arrange an appointment for me? If you're the one to set it up, he might be more amenable to discussing your case with me."

Frankie hailed Willy again and said nothing until the new drinks were poured.

"I followed his instructions to a T and got ripped off for $10,000. It all happened in just 45 minutes. How could that happen if the place was honest?"

Frankie had a point. Was he pigeon-holed as a naïve rich kid the moment he entered? Maybe the broker sized him up on the spot and decided to hit him hard right off the bat, the rationale being that the sucker wouldn't be coming back for more. They could make more money off him than a hundred regular clients and do it in time for late afternoon celebration at the speak down on Beaver Street.

Humph drained his glass and stood.

"I'm off to see your guy. He probably has a lot of dinner jackets by now. On Park Avenue, right?"

"Right." Frankie suddenly looked depressed. Maybe it was shame for having been screwed over by Tom, Dick and Harry. He didn't get up to show Humph to the door.

"Good day to you, Sir Humph," said William as the detective made his escape.

Just before the door closed behind him, Humph heard Frankie:

"Willy!"

If Frankie started boozing this early in the day, thought Humph, he'd be the easiest mark Wall Street ever saw.

CHAPTER 4

HUMPH, with two Scotches under his belt, was dozing off when the train reached the 67th Street station. All he had to do was walk five or six blocks to get to the address he'd been given on Park Avenue. Once the corporate headquarters of an oil baron, it had been converted into an enormous luxury building. Even judging by outside appearances, Humph was certain the building had never before rented to an office clerk. Humph would love to see what the man put down as employment on his rental application.

The doorman almost smirked at the sight of Humph's well-worn wool suit before verifying that apartment 27 was expecting a visitor.

"Have you been here before, sir?"

"No."

"It can be confusing... although the layout is one of the features that sets this building apart. Let me show you the way."

Humph followed the gaunt-faced doorman's measured strides past a hallway leading to apartments. That made Humph think he would be directed to take the elevator to another floor. The doorman walked right by the elevator and led Humph through double doors leading to what appeared to be a garden. Only then did he realize that there was a courtyard with park-like greenery, shrubs, young trees and tidy flower beds. Rows of benches stretched the entire length of the block-long building. There were also spots where long-snouted luxury automobiles could park at an angle. The doorman pointed across the way to the entrance to Apartment 27, on the ground floor.

"In case you were wondering, you can walk on the grass."

Grass. It was a foreign word in Humph's neighborhood.

Before proceeding to the business at hand, Humph availed himself of a bench. The wooden slats were varnished so thickly they were almost mirrors. No risk of splinters, he noted in his obsessively observational way.

He was perspiring slightly from the unaccustomed morning whiskey and his brisk walk to Park Avenue. He also surmised that just being on Park Avenue from the low 30s to the 70s could have that effect on mortals.

What did he want to learn from the wonder boy clerk? Logic and process always calmed him down. He unbuttoned the tight vest under his suit jacket. He also felt like unbuttoning his shirt for a moment or two. That would probably be scandalous in this world, he decided.

If the clerk was a straight shooter, Humph was sure he could advance his investigation. If he'd learned too much about condescending misdirection from his former boss, Frankie's dad, Humph would have to lower his expectations. If the clerk didn't help him, Humph's only resort was to go to a shabby-looking brokerage and pretend to be a hick with a $20 or $30 wad to invest. Since he knew little about investing, he realized with relief that he wouldn't have to do a lot of acting.

To his immense surprise, the clerk himself answered the door after ringing Humph in. Obviously, Frankie had kept his word and "warned" the clerk about the visitor he was sending his way. To round out the surprise, the clerk extended his hand and said, "Pleasure to meet you, sir."

He led Humph into his living room. Despite the kid's wealth, he didn't have a taste for the exotic. Landscape paintings, which Humph always found boring, 19th-century chairs and sofas, which Humph deeply appreciated since they offered comfort for outsized people.

"Tea, juice, a drink?"

"Juice. Thank you." It would revive him for what now promised to be an interesting interrogation.

The clerk returned.

"Apparently we are out of juice. The maid, I'm told, is shopping at this very moment. In the meantime, I found some icy-cold lemonade. Humph accept the glass gladly.

"I neglected to introduce myself. Colin Lenester, of Philadelphia. There are a lot of Lenesters there." He said it with a self-deprecating smile.

Humph already liked him. Not ideal for an interrogation, however. Liking someone could easily lead to them hoodwinking you.

Humph drained half the lemonade in one go, then posed a question. He decided to be straight forward. No beating around the bush. No intent to trick the young man.

"What puzzles me, Mr. Lenester, is first of all, how a young man with no investing experience or expertise, according to Frankie, could walk into a clip joint and walk out with a fortune. To be frank, Mr. Lenester, I would dearly love to know the secret. I desperately need the wherewithal to buy a light-weight suit."

Lenester laughed. He clearly loved the question, which he surely anticipated.

"The answer, Mr. Detective, is that while I did win a little money on my first go-around at a brokerage... I think I put down $10 and left with $72 once I'd paid broker fees. To me that was a stupendous amount. Frankie's dad paid me $172.50 a month, and that was the recompense for a senior clerk. Despite my youth, I was a senior clerk. I achieved that rank because I worked as if a guillotine were hanging from the ceiling directly above me."

He then mentioned that he grew up in the Five Points.

"When I was 14, my father found out what a dagger in his throat felt like. The dagger was a reward for involving himself with the wife of a neighborhood bully. As for my mother, she died when I was 17 from syphilis passed on by our landlord in our very bedroom in return for a month's missed rent.

"So, sir, don't confuse me with the likes of Frankie. To not put too fine a point on it, I bear a hatred for him and every one of his companions."

Humph was speechless. He'd never dealt with a Park Avenue witness or suspect before. He imagined they would all pull social rank, politely obfuscate and then shoo him away.

"I confess to be a tad taken aback by your declaration. It's very much appreciated. However, is it too late to accept your offer of a drink?"

Mr. Lenester nodded his understanding. This time he called the maid. Humph had heard her enter a moment before by another door. There was no more need for Lenester to pretend. He was rich without a doubt but he had proved to be the man he'd always been. He instinctively knew Humph understood.

"On my second visit to a broker, the same one that enriched my life with the equivalent of half a month's pay in return for no labor, I offered to buy him a beer after work.

It was Son of a B of a sultry day and he accepted. I explained my beginnings in life and my current job situation."

Lenester said it became clear in only minutes that the broker never knew the joy of having a silver spoon in his youth. His childhood, he said, was simple at best, infinitely boring, and not at all promising. One thing the broker did have was a head for figures. He failed most of his classes in his first and final year of college but a professor repeatedly told him he would have every right to dream of being an accountant. Everything about the young man's family was drenched in Protestant pragmatism. No one said dreaming wasn't allowed but he was never encouraged to indulge in pointless imaginings. Accordingly, he ignored the professor's advice and began the hunt for a job that required a two-plus-two wizard. He worked briefly doing books for a grocery store. It provided long hours of boredom, during which he would read the papers, which were on sale at a stand just outside the store, right next to the bins of dill pickles and cured frankfurters.

"That, Mr. Detective…"

"Please do me the honor of calling me Humph. No misters, no detective."

"As I was going to say, Humph, that was where the young broker-to-be learned to dream for the first time in his life. Almost every day he read about ordinary guys like him striking it rich on the stock market."

He said that one Sunday he made his way to Wall Street. He said he wished he had a camera. Sundays in the financial district were as peaceful and quiet as a Hudson Valley meadow. He would have photographed every building and hung the pictures on the walls of his room. He said he felt excited for the first time in his life.

"He said he feigned illness not long afterwards and spent three days knocking on brokerage doors. Two places were interested in hiring him but had nothing immediately available. A third, however, interviewed him at length. They tested him by throwing investing terminology at him after the briefest of explanations about what they meant for the investor and, more importantly what they meant for the brokerage."

The young man told Lenester he had no trouble figuring out payments minus sliding-scale commissions, how much a percentage point change in a stock's direction had significance for the investor, and how much to push the investor if necessary.

"He was hired on the spot."

After a moment, Lenester added: "From that moment on, I couldn't help wondering whether I might someday have a shot at becoming a big shot."

Lenester was clearly embarrassed by that admission, which added to the esteem Humph had already accumulated for the young man.

"Who wouldn't be excited at that possibility," Humph said, hoping he'd continue.

"Well, for your edification, here's what the kid told me he did for starters. His first job was as a quotation board guy. He had to post prices on the board in what they called the customer's room. The customers got all excited by being in that room and sitting near the stock ticker. They would hear prices being called out non-stop. They'd feel part of something big and great. They felt part of the force that drove America, even though they were nobodies who didn't even have a bank account, and maybe not even a grade-school education. An investor, they figured, was anyone's equal, top hat or no. Just gotta love democracy."

Lenester then explained that when the kid started to feel something in his pants packets beside his privates, he would go out on his own and invest in what are called "bucket shops". The place he worked in was on the up and up for the most part. Not so with bucket shops.

"I've been told about them," said Humph, happy to show he wasn't full-blown ignorant.

Because the kid knew enough not to be duped, Lenester said, he soon became more than modestly successful.

"That's when I started funding him," Lenester said. "How could the kid resist? He was now running no risk at all and I gave him 20 percent of the profit he made me. 'Best job I ever had,' he told me."

Lenester said the kid became so good at it that a lot of bucket shops refused to take his money. They'd lost too many times.

"This is where the straight-as-an-arrow piece of nothing started to really shine. Life was becoming fun as well as profitable. He went to a burlesque show and collared one of the performers after the show. He wanted to learn everything about make-up."

Lenester went on to explain that the kid would disguise himself so the bucket shop guys wouldn't recognize him.

"And it worked. He would start small buying maybe just a dozen shares of this or that. And he'd do it like a yokel. He lost on purpose. Then a few weeks later he'd go back. They'd welcome him like a long-lost buddy. Before they knew what happened, he'd used his knowledge of how certain stocks behave from one day to the next, how they responded to sudden selling or buying, and before they knew what hit them, he'd scored big at their expense. He'd become persona non grata—I've never said anything in Latin before—everywhere."

Lenester said more than anything it was the arrangement with the kid that made him rich. To become gloriously rich, he started investing with bank brokers. He was now respectable because he could afford a good suit and put real money on the table. The growth rate was on the conservative side but like the guys he read about in the society columns, Lenester was in the game for the long haul. It didn't take long before the corporate con artists were sending insider tips his way.

Humph raised his glass to life without guillotines.

"The best toast ever," said the former clerk.

The maid, who'd been listening, also wore a big smile as she showed Humph out.

Humph's face wasn't constructed in a way that permitted certain expressions. The large forehead, the small eyes, the almost muscular cheek bones, the tree trunk neck, all set on a massive pedestal, didn't invite representations of simple delight. Yet, as he stepped back onto Park Avenue, delight was what he felt. Lenester was more accommodating than Humph could have imagined. Humph was feeling damn near playful. "If I find myself another drink or two," Humph mused, "I just might drop a mention to someone in a saloon that I had a friend on Park Avenue."

It was too late in the day to explore the address where Frankie said he was ripped off. Besides, before doing that, Humph wanted to try his luck in a bucket shop, to see if his insider information would lead to a winning investment. That would wait until tomorrow. For now, the mission was to seek out Eve. She deserved some kind of reward for the leads she'd given him. What mattered to him was the feeling he and Eve, his one love's daughter, were working together on a case. Selfish as the thought was, he wished he could contrive a reason for her to keep working with him.

When he got to her place, on Forsyth Street, just below Delancey, a man answered her door.

'Where's Eve?"

"Who the hell are you?"

"Family. Where's Eve?"

The guy, a young man who looked as if he probably packed a good punch, told Humph that she'd had an accident.

"Details, kid, or I'll bring the cops. I used to be one so they'll be at this door real fast."

Humph didn't have to raise his voice. His size and a baritone voice that flirted with the upper bass range usually had a commanding effect. In winter, when an overcoat allowed him to conceal it, he carried his old police baton, a one-foot length of hardwood headache. If his suit jacket weren't so snug, he'd carry it year long. In his hard-drinking days on the force, Humph referred to the baton as his Bowery buddy.

The kid at the door saw reason and answered Humph's question, sort of.

"Eve didn't come home last night. I have no idea where she went because she's out of work until next week. There's a new show..."

Humph cut him off. He knew her work routine. She was either stripping or working burlesque. She'd described the situation on her last visit.

"Has she talked about anyone she might know on Wall Street lately?"

The kid was silent for a long minute. Humph didn't think he was being evasive. The young man's furrowed brow was for real as he racked his brain. Finally, he spoke.

"Don't know if this is important but... First, sorry, but would you like to come in?

One glance with his practiced eye told Humph that everything in Eve's apartment appeared as it should, orderly disorder. Humph sometimes surmised that the state of Eve's apartment might represent her proud, 1920s-liberated-woman defiance. He didn't know much about that attitude but the *New Yorker* talked about it all the time now. Eve's main job in life wasn't and never would be housekeeping.

Humph promptly dropped himself down onto a leather hassock, making himself less intimidating. He wanted to make it easy for the kid.

"Some guy called on her a day or two ago. I was just leaving so I didn't pay much attention. All I remember was that he was short. He had a paunch. His face was kind of fat, too. Eve knew him. You could tell. I remember she called him by name at the door. By the way she was standing, her legs apart like she was getting ready to brace herself, it made it obvious that she wasn't going to let him in. That's when I squeezed by the two of them to go to work I remember she said, 'What the hell do you want, Reggie?'"

Humph raised his hand, telling the kid to stop talking. "Reggie, Reggie?" Then it came to him: Reginald, Reginald Ostenbruch, pronounced Osten Brook. The pontifical broker Eve threatened to betray if he refused to see Humph. Humph had to find him. He rose and took the kid's hand.

"Thanks. Thanks a million."

The kid was surprised how fast a man that size could get out the door and head up the street.

When Humph got to the fat little man's brokerage, he learned he hadn't shown up yet. The secretary said that wasn't unusual, although he did show up most days.

"Would you like to see another broker, sir?"

"Would you have his home address? It's important that I see him."

"I'm sorry. I not allowed to divulge that."

Humph was standing beside her. He put his big paw lightly on her shoulder and thanked her anyway.

"But," she hurried to say, blushing slightly at his touch, "I know that he lives in Gramercy Park on East 18th Street. We, I mean the staff, we were once invited there to celebrate July 4th. I don't remember the address but there was the nicest little garden in the back."

Humph touched her shoulder again, thanked her and left.

Just as he closed the door behind him, the secretary called out, "Sir! Sir." She hurried to the door and, fortunately for her, found Humph leaning against the building as he wrote in a small notepad with a pencil stub.

"Sir, sir."

Humph turned.

"I just found this envelope under a pile of papers on my desk. It must be Mr. Ostenbruch's home address right there on the front of it. It might be a summary of his remuneration at the brokerage for the last quarter. Perhaps you could take it to him."

What a perfect entrée, thought Humph.

This time he placed a hand on each of her shoulders and heartily thanked her.

"Come back anytime, sir, if you have more questions that is."

The address on East 18th was between Second and Third avenues. Tired and tense because of Eve's disappearance, he hailed a cab.

The tidy row of red brick townhouses looked idyllic. Trees, flower boxes, freshly painted, low, black wrought-iron fencing. Some windows were stained glass.

The door knocker was brass and surprisingly heavy. Two minutes later, he rapped again, this time harder. Finally, a maid answered.

"*Señor Osten, sí. Momento por favor.*"

Convenient, thought Humph. "No English, *no comprendo nada.*"

Even if she spoke English, she'd undoubtedly be under orders to comprender nada.

For a split second, Humph wondered why was he assuming the guy was dishonest or dangerous? He decided to rein himself in. He suspected the worst because he instinctively disliked the guy. That wouldn't stand up in court. Humph disliked his mailman, so cool it, he told himself again.

When Señor Oster appeared, his mouth smiled but his eyes betrayed alarm.

"Mr. Humph. Have I got the right?"

Humph didn't bother to correct him.

"I'm looking for a friend. I've been led to believe that you can help me. Where is a lovely young lady named Eve? I don't think I need remind you of how you and I first met, I mean the person who facilitated our get-together, and the reason she was able to get you to agree to see me."

"Please come in, Mr. Humph."

He led the way to the living room. It was immaculate. The tin ceiling was painted white. The floors were dark-stained hardwood, a beautiful contrast with the ceiling, almost a heaven-and-hell arrangement. Two windows let in the day's sunshine and looked out on the garden, the one the secretary had referred to. Whether Ostenbruch, or whatever his name was, was honest or not, he lived a Manhattan dream life.

Humph wanted to ask him if his place had hot water but restrained himself.

"Eve. Yes, Eve. Lovely young woman. I did see her on the day you mentioned. We had a matter to discuss. I'm afraid she wasn't in the best of moods."

"What did you discuss?"

The broker pretended he was working hard to recall, as if a visit from a looker like Eve was an everyday occurrence.

"Work. That's right. She said she was out of work of late and she wondered whether, with all my connections I might know of any opportunities."

He left the statement hanging. It would have been logical for him to tell Humph how he replied to the young woman's question. Apparently, the broker had to work hard to remember that as well. Or was he working hard to fabricate the conversation?

"Sorry, Mr. Humph. My mind wandered for a moment. Yes, I recall that she wanted regular work as a dancer. I was able to inform her that I knew the owners of several establishments which engage dancers and other entertainers. Your Eve was clearly relieved by my answer. Yes, I remember that well. It felt rather pleasant to be a good Samaritan as it were."

"I don't imagine you get to feel like that very often on Wall Street," Humph said.

The broker laughed. "Can't deny that, sir."

He said he didn't know what Eve finally decided to do.

Humph asked him for the names of the owners of

the places he recommended to Eve. The broker had a coughing fit.

"*Agua! Agua!*" he called to the maid. In no time at all, she appeared with a jug of ice water and a glass, which she poured as if serving royalty.

When he recovered, the broker mumbled the names of some clubs, but not their owners. Humph knew he wasn't likely to get their names from the broker without making the interview unpleasant. He stood and told the broker he'd see himself out. By the time he reached the door, the maid had caught up with him and reached in front of him to take the doorknob.

"Gooood day, meester."

Humph hoped the bastard paid her as if she were a handful of maids. He didn't deserve royal treatment.

Home was now the only thing on Humph's mind. At least he had leads as to Eve's possible whereabouts. At a newsstand, the headlines of each paper proclaimed, "Sacco and Vanzetti Executed". So much for the anarchists, Humph thought, if that's what they were. He wasn't sure. A towering wave of anti-immigrant, anti-Italian feeling was sweeping the city and it had clearly soaked the jury in the Sacco and Vanzetti case. Appeals were all denied. No one realistically expected them to be upheld in this political climate. As a cop, Humph and his colleagues knew they had free rein when subduing suspected wrongdoers if they were immigrants. After all, his sergeant would say, "They're all bomb-throwing anarchists, right? It's in their blood."

As a beat cop, Humph got to know a lot of Italians. The worst crime most of them were guilty of was the same as anyone of European origin: they made their own wine and beer just as their ancestors did, a time-honored reward for a long day of work for starvation wages. Humph had even heard that thousands of them were giving up on the American dream and returning to Europe just because of the insanity called Prohibition that had infected Americans for the past seven years.

Humph had been at the head of the line when speakeasies started to open by the thousands in New York. Most New Yorkers despised Prohibition but the Dry side got most of the headlines. Many of the Dry proponents, Humph knew all too well, were anti-immigrant of any kind. Their prejudice was their religion. Every time he read about them in the paper, he had an urge to drink.

Humph found a nickel on the sidewalk and used it to take a trolley home. He opened his paper and read the accounts of the execution. By the time he got to Worth Street and Chatham Square he had a thirst on. He headed up the street to a speak that had replaced the bar he and his cop cohorts frequented at shift's end. Prohibition agents had missed this bar. Their task was outrageously impossible, Humph decided when a report posted on a bulletin board at his precinct station years ago said that only 50 agents had been assigned to New York. The city had by all accounts more than 30,000 speakeasies. The agents tried valiantly to impose Prohibition on the city but only a handful of cases ever went to court. Clubs would frequently get shut down, only to reopen at another location, often with a different name. Humph more than once had marveled at how loyal customers figured out where the new locations were in time for opening night just days after the first placed was shuttered.

At worst, club owners and others charged with violating the Eighteenth Amendment to the Constitution paid fines of $25. Since mobsters were behind a lot of the clubs, the fines were mere specks of dust on their spats. Those charged were so numerous they left the courts paralyzed. Hearings were held with 200 defendants at a time. Even the New York State legislature said to hell with the nonsense and repealed the state's "dry" law. Even though the federal Prohibition Act was still the law of the land, New York had made a statement. It was proud to be the country's No. 1 wet city.

Humph's cop colleagues kept making thousands of liquor busts a year for the sole purpose of eliciting bribes and confiscating booze for the boys in blue.

Humph was hoping some of his cop buddies would be at the bar. Sober or not, they had brains worth picking, he figured. He needed to know which gangsters ran which clubs. If the broker was as successful as his Gramercy Park townhouse suggested, his connections were at high levels.

Humph was in good spirits by the time the cops started to roll in. The older ones said the giant's surprise appearance was worth a celebration all by itself. A chorus of "I'm buying" or "I'm buying the next two" broke out, like investors screaming to the brokerage boys with chalk in their hands to record their buy offers.

Almost everyone in the speak was a cop. Nothing really changes, Humph thought. The friendly pounding his back was taking almost made him forget how he'd grown to hate the job as well as the things they'd stooped to do that were far beyond the law. For the most part, they were no better than the street gangs that scared protection money out of starving vegetable and fruit vendors on the Lower East Side.

As late afternoon eased into early evening, the boozy debate over who the biggies were started to find agreement when names like Luciano, Costello and Rothstein were mentioned.

Did the slimy little broker actually count them as friends? If he did, thought Humph through the fog of brew and blue, he wouldn't have to reach that high to steal away Eve. He needed underlings, the people who made the mob operations hum. How to broach the subject without make it sound like something that involved him personally?

"A round for everyone," Humph cried, his own glass raised high like a Roman Legionnaire's standard. In his head, he was thinking, "Come to Caesar, boys."

He immediately bit his tongue. Too much damn reading for his own good.

"Boys," he said, standing to get everyone's attention, "a dear friend of mine, a young lady, if you know what I mean, has been kidnapped. The man I suspect of having arranged the nap is untouchable. I spent an hour with him this afternoon and got absolutely nowhere. He's got protection from his asshole to his yapper and he knows it. I think my young friend tried to extort money from him for past wrongs. There's no need to go into detail except to say he cornered her after she did a suggestive dance one night in a burlesque production. She was just earning a living and doing so honestly. He kept coming back to see her and she let him think they were friends with possibilities. After all, he paid handsomely for the slightest flirtation."

There was a ripple of agreement. They all knew how things worked.

"Finally, although the decision was not the wisest thing to do, she decided to squeeze him for some serious money. He had abused her on several occasions and she wanted him to pay. You know the way young ladies are these days. They don't take crap."

The remark first produced laughter. Then the bar went silent, all ears taking in the giant's words. What he said didn't really matter. He was still a brother in blue.

"My young friend has not returned home since he visited her, uninvited, three days ago. My gut tells me he saw a lithe dancer's body he could sell and thereby exact revenge for her temerity."

A cop blurted out, "What's temerity mean?"

Seeing how drunk the guy was, Humph replied simply:

"It means balls."

The question, Humph explained was, "Who could he have sold her to? A dance hall, a speak, a house of prostitution? Which buyer would pay the most money for a young lady like that? Remember, this man is connected. He thinks the world of himself. And I'll wager my best boots that he's as vindictive as...." Again he bit his tongue. He was about to say Hera, a Greek goddess married to the philandering god Zeus. "...as vindictive as a woman betrayed by her lifetime-long lover."

Humph went for a leak. When he returned, the room was buzzing, interrupted only by clarion calls for more beer. Their enthusiasm amazed Humph. Their sergeant never inspired them to such heights. It occurred to Humph that these coppers had no idea of how much he despised their job. He had taken it for granted that by abandoning ship almost in mid-shift, the message would have been clear. They certainly weren't loyal to their job of being law-abiding and law-enforcing cops. But maybe they possessed the quality of loyalty when it came to their own. It was hard not to admire.

Several of his brothers in blue pushed to the front of the group, facing Humph directly. He guessed they were the default spokesmen.

"Humph, it appears we might be able to help you out. We put our heads together at your request and here is what we came up with."

They said they had several theories.

"First, there was a great likelihood that they have sold your friend to a brothel as a prostitute. That would be very bad news because she would be imprisoned in that brothel, which is undoubtedly gang operated.

"If your broker bastard wants to humiliate her, that's what he'd do. Any of his mob friends, big or small, would welcome the gift of a young body."

After a long pause, which allowed Humph to resurface after hearing the horrific picture they'd drawn, they added:

"We have three names. You should start there."

The names included one minor mobster Humph had heard of, one he hadn't and a woman he had. His boys knew their clubs. One of them wrote their addresses on the back of a two-day old newspaper they'd found in the can.

CHAPTER 5

HUMPH left the bar and headed due south to Henry Street and home. Though he was walking south and, thanks to being pickled, he was relieved that south from anywhere meant downhill, as in "go down to the Equator", he strode like a runaway horse. Zigs got interspersed with dangerous zags. He paused at a lamp post and told himself he'd have to work on his booze capacity. It had diminished greatly since his days in uniform. As he pushed away from the post and resumed his journey home, he replayed the new clues. He indeed had something to investigate. Once home, he didn't bother to undress. He didn't want to interrupt his thoughts. He was asleep before the lack of logic became apparent.

The next morning, urgent knocking at his door woke him. Could it be Eve? He hurried to open it, stubbing his toe on a chair on the way. The pain only surfaced when he saw the male face in his doorway. It was not Eve's. It was a cop, one of his drinking buddies from the night before.

The cop walked in behind Humph and sat at the table while the big man bent to the floor to massage his stubbed toe. When he finished and raised his head, a wave of dizziness welcomed him to the new day.

"So, Charles Duffy," said Humph, "if you're here to continue drinking, the answer is no."

The cop smiled sympathetically.

"No, I'm here because some of the lads and I put our heads together after you left. Detective Rankin, you remember him, the fat, fat one, he and another dick came in and we picked their brains as well. Came up with a couple of possibilities for you."

That was damned nice of them, Humph thought, but their kindness to a former cop reminded him of one of the reasons he left the force. Last night, he got fried in less than three hours. The others must have carried on for at least a few more. That nightly routine had been Humph's as well and it had been killing him. And who knows whether they'd stopped drinking after leaving the speak last night.

Thanks to Prohibition enforcement seizures, the precinct station was as well stocked as many small bars were. The bottles were all kept down in the station's basement, in a storage room next to the furnace. Hung on the door was a sign that read Evidence Locker #2. The letters were written in multi-colored crayon, as a child might do. Humph remembered fetching bottles from the room in the past and having to blow off the coal dust before bringing them back upstairs for the boys.

Officer Duffy said one of the detectives knew a certain Mr. Reginald Ostenbruch. He said he couldn't pin anything on him yet but he knew the broker was chummy with none other than Owney Madden.

Humph didn't need to be told who Madden was. An Irish-born mobster who held the reins of a whole lot of the Prohibition enterprises, from the ones that imported booze to the ones that provided posh spots to consume it in. Madden and both respectable and not so respectable investors were behind a host of clubs, including celebrity clubs like the Cotton Club in Harlem to a handful of clip joints scattered throughout Manhattan.

"The good detective asked me to impart to you a couple of his theories."

"Sure you don't want a drink to welcome 12 bells, or anything else that comes to mind?" Humph's hangover was disappearing at the possibility of getting a lead about Eve's fate. Humph knew he didn't have to ask twice. Using his long arm to reach to the back of the highest cupboard in the kitchen, the kind of place some people used to hide their piggy banks, Humph grasped a bottle of Irish whiskey. Alongside it, he plunked down two shot glasses that had been hidden in his huge left hand.

After filling each, Humph sat and faced Duffy.

"Cheers," he said, raising a glass. "Kindly now impart."

The officer chuckled.

"We miss you, you big oaf."

"Talk."

"OK. The detective said that broker fella has been known to assist Mr. Madden in obtaining girls for his clubs."

"What kind of girls?" Humph was about to burst out that Eve was no whore but that wouldn't be quite true. He decided to let Duffy finish.

Duffy noticed Humph's fists as they twitched suddenly, only to relax just as fast. He stared at Humph. Duffy wasn't big but he was as wiry as a Kansas farmer. All muscle, a handy attribute on the beat around the Bowery. Humph knew the officer wasn't preparing to defend himself. Like any good cop, he was just observant.

"The broker bastard, what he apparently does is talk up the opportunities available for a talented and beautiful dancer or entertainer in one of Madden's places. Better bucks than burlesque, long-term contracts, the whole kit and caboodle.

"You say he once got fresh with your Eve and she set him good and straight afterwards. Sounds like he'd want to show her who's boss. But to pull it off, without giving the young lady cause to seek you out again, Humph, he set her up with something irresistible. You said she needed work the last time you saw her. Maybe the Brook fella offered to pay her rent or he offered her a grand job. So let's say, she goes off with him on the day in question. Obviously, she hasn't come back.

"To cut things short, our detective Rankin suggests that maybe she's now under Madden's thumb, so to speak. He has some pretty wild women running his high-class speaks. They are flapper girls personified, the ones who don't take any mouth from men, maybe even mobsters. One was a movie actress who liked to ride wild horses and shoot a gun while doing it. Guess she decided the soft life in New York was better than fame that came along with being saddle sore. There's another speakeasy queen who apparently used to be something or other in a touring Wild West show in Texas before she got the hankerin'…"

"You're sounding more like a cowhand by the minute," Humph interrupted while filling their glasses again. "And I am more than a little impressed by your use of 'impart'. Hankerin' and impartin'. Juries would like that. Good homespun speakin'."

"Always trying to better myself, Humph," the officer said, unable to hold back a grin. "Anyway, as I was saying, she got the hankerin' to come to New York.

"On the surface, Humph, there's nothing much scary about the idea of working with a woman, but your Eve wouldn't have a clue about how those gals work, and she wouldn't know that they in turn work for a big-time gangster. Humph, I think you can imagine that these aren't necessarily the kind of jobs that let you return to home sweet home when your night's done. The detective suggested that maybe that's why you haven't seen your girl since she went off with the broker guy."

Humph hated to admit it but the theory the detective gave Duffy sounded plausible.

Like a well-choreographed move, the cop and the former cop drained their glasses at exactly the same moment.

"I'm going to check out Eve's place now just in case there's news from her boyfriend. You're welcome to tag along."

Duffy poured himself another shot, downed it while standing and joined Humph at the door.

When they got to Eve's flat there was no one home. Humph, however, had a key, which Eve had made for him after an evening of discussing his most dangerous cases.

"If things get too hot, Humph, you could always hole up at my place," she said long ago. "They'd never find you there." The truth was, Humph had several times fallen afoul of some of the toughs in the old Five Points streets. When he was a cop in uniform, they figured it might be unwise to beat the pudding out of him but now the private dick in street clothes was fair game. Humph could hold his own in a fight but the boys down there preferred to work in groups.

Humph didn't usually go into detail about his cases but that evening had been different. He had gone to a theater to watch Eve do some song and dance numbers, then turn up the heat with a first-rate burlesque tease that was both sensual and tongue in cheek. He had insisted on celebrating her performance with a drink at his place. He had all but abandoned the idea of going to shows after losing his love but he was glad Eve had insisted.

"You are badly in need of having fun, Humph!" Little Eve had all but dragged huge Humph to Broadway for the show. Afterwards, she was glad he'd seen how professional she was on stage, the way her mother had been.

Over time, she started pecking for details about his private-eye work. Humph always said it was boring but Eve found his cases exciting.

When he and Officer Duffy entered Eve's place, Humph snapped back to the present. It was clear that Eve hadn't returned. Everything of Eve's was exactly the way she'd left them days before. Her boyfriend obviously didn't feel free to put her clothes away and tidy up the place.

The trip wasn't a waste of time because as awful as the idea of Eve being kidnapped was, he had to be sure she was gone before he could investigate, especially now that he knew some gangland heavyweights might be involved, either first-hand or peripherally.

"Would your Eve have gone willingly with the broker?" Duffy asked.

"Not unless she was chasing him with a baseball bat."

The two started knocking on doors of apartments in Eve's building, then repeated the same futile exercise up the street where the boyfriend said the broker had driven away with Eve. After an hour, they retraced their steps on the way back to Humph's place. Duffy had decided not to go to work. Too little sleep. Too much firewater. "Can I pass out at your place, Humph?"

The constable fell asleep on Humph's bed. Although Humph had said he wanted to do some thinking, he fell asleep sitting ramrod straight in his chair. It was a skill he learned as a cop. He developed it after hearing from soldiers who fought in the Great War. They said they'd get so desperate for sleep they learned to fall asleep standing up leaning against a building or the side of a trench.

CHAPTER 6

THE next day, Humph was even more paralyzed with worry about Eve. He was tempted to go back to the two-faced broker's office and, if that failed, his home in Gramercy Park. He'd squat on the doorstep if necessary. The adrenalin was pumping. Not a good thing, Humph had learned through past investigations. Clarity, observation, thoroughness, objectivity. He could go on listing how best to investigate. He realized he had to pull himself together. Good, good, he told himself as he became Humph the dick and not Humph the surrogate father of Eve. Good, he told himself again.

"Shit!" he said out loud a few seconds later.

He had a case to solve, one that would pay the rent. He'd almost forgotten about the rich kid who'd hired him to get his investment losses back, or at least find out who'd screwed him out of all that dough. Humph had to start investing today to find out how brokers hoodwinked the bumpkins and labor-weary New Yorkers who managed to throw together a few bucks. They were as ignorant about investing as he was before seeing Eve's broker client.

The first place he went to was a hole-in-the-wall brokerage on Broad Street. He chose it as a starting place because it looked so in need of investment itself. Narrow store front, dirty single window, drab to the core, all except for cheap but colorful wooden signs wherever there was no glass.

They read:

"We dream too. Come on in!"

"You, too, can hold your head high like a banker!"

"The best margins in town."

"Who needs cash? We don't. See for yourself."

Coney Island barkers sounded a hundred times more legit. A great place to start, thought Humph. This must be what they call a bucket shop. The bastard broker had told him they were all gone but Humph had found a story in the paper that said they were still around but far fewer in number.

He stepped inside and was greeted immediately.

"Step right this way, sir."

They entered a low-ceilinged room with two desks and several chairs. Signs on the wall parroted those on the outside of the building.

"May I ask for a few particulars, sir?"

Humph didn't say no so the man continued.

"Care to sit while we chat?" The man was behind Humph in a second, edging a chair against the back of Humph's knees, almost forcing him to sit.

"First of all, you look like you're astute enough to be a Wall Street veteran but if by chance you're not, I'm sure you will appreciate an explanation of the first steps on the road to rich." The man chuckled to show his hyperbole was harmless.

"Proceed, sir," said Humph.

Humph was astounded that the man had the nerve to greedily rub his hands together and meet Humph's stare head-on.

"How much were you considering as an investment today?"

"Very little, to be honest. I am, as they say in baseball, a rookie."

"Well, sir, you've chosen the best place in all of New York to begin your new life. Let me explain ever so briefly. We will even accept, from a sincere newcomer such as yourself, an investment of a mere $10. Nothing to be ashamed of. You are not the first. However, what makes your decision to choose this establishment so fortuitous is that we will double your investment at no cost to you. If you invest wisely today, that means you can make double the money, again at no cost to you. Can you beat that?" The man rattled on at such a breakneck speed that Humph almost felt he was truly riding a wave to success.

"What are margins?" Humph asked.

"Ah, excellent. A man who has done his research. OK, margins are simply the name we give the money we give to you to give you a chance to win big. For example, you are considering a newcomer's bet of $10. We'll throw in $10 to double the stakes. That money, our money, the brokerage's money, is what's called a margin.

Humph knew enough to know that the brokerage wasn't giving him the $10. It was a loan. He had learned that the brokerage was sharing in his investment. If it goes well, no problem. The brokerage makes a profit just like he will. If it doesn't, the brokerage can do what it wants with the stock he bought. It can even sell it and he would have no say in the stock in which he had invested $10. If the stock loses money, he would not only lose the $10 he'd bet. He would also have to pay back the $10 loan he was supposed to think was a gift, and he'd have to pay interest on that amount.

Humph was starting to feel sorry for his client, the arrogant rich kid.

"OK," he said. "Let's invest my $10 and the $10 you're giving me, right?"

"Correct, sir. The next step is to choose a stock to invest in. Please step this way."

They entered a much larger room with a high ceiling. Humph found himself staring at a big chalk board and some kind of machine on the right-hand side.

"What's that?" he asked, pointing.

"That is our link to the world of money, sir. It's called a stock ticker. What it tells us about investments taking place in the most important companies in America is exactly what bankers see in their own investment houses. What stocks are increasing in value, which ones are declining as people buy and sell today. Come, take a seat by the ticker and then watch the quote boys enter the latest values on the big board in front of you. It's really quite exciting."

Humph, giving the impression of being transfixed by the big board, smiled and said, "I have to agree!"

The man excused himself, mercifully, for several minutes while he tended to two new walk-ins. Humph wasn't quite sure of what he was seeing being written hastily on the big board for his stock. He hated fractions.

When the man returned he clapped Humph on the back and announced:

"Time to put your money down. Come with me."

They went to the back of what they called the customer room and stuck their heads through a cubbyhole. A clerk appeared momentarily. No smile. Humph's overall impression was "mechanical". The clerk reached out his hand for the money, the investment.

"Buying or selling, sir?"

The clerk looked at the quotation board and took the price from there — the last one. Humph observed that he also put down the time on the ticket so that it showed that they had bought or sold for Humph X number of shares of stock X at X price at X time on X day and how much money they received from Humph. It all looked so above board.

"You, sir, are now participant in the great American money-maker known as Wall Street!"

Humph, at his humble best, asked if he could remain for a while to watch the progress of his investment.

"What a request!" said the carney broker. "We encourage such participation. Why, sir? Because you will begin to see magic at work. You will become addicted to the magic of money. Guaranteed."

Two and a half hours later, when Humph's behind could take no more of the small wooden chair he was provided with, he sought out the agent of his new-found fortune.

"Sir," he said, making an effort not to allow his voice to descend to its natural bottom-range notes, "I have difficulty translating these numbers and fractions into results. Have I made or lost money?"

The agent grabbed the ticket from Humph's fingertips and a second later declared:

"You, sir, are a winner. My God, for a first investment, rarely have I seen such pristine instinct. Your $10 is now worth no less than $42. Shall I figure out the percentage of your profit? It's more than 400 percent. Do you need to sit a moment to take it all in, your good fortune?"

Humph acquiesced. Part of him didn't believe his windfall for a minute. Another part said, "But what if this really happened? After all, all the stories of rags to riches say…"

His sore ass suddenly restored him to reality.

He returned to the cubbyhole and shoved his investment slip to the morose clerk. In seconds, he had $42 cash in hand. He turned to thank the agent but he was already busy with new potential customers.

Once outside, Humph headed north to the *New York World* Building on Park Row. The paper was famous for something called "yellow journalism" but it had some of the city's top reporters. One of them, Gerald Franklin, was a friend when Franklin was just a cub reporter. He was always respectful at crime scenes and Humph eventually gave him access to insider information. The reporter was grateful. His star had risen, just like his paycheck thanks to Humph.

Tired of sitting on his butt at the brokerage, if that is what it was, Humph had speed-walked the dozen or so blocks up to Park Row. When he arrived, sweating, the doorman and the security guard he'd been chatting with weren't going to let him in. When Humph mentioned the name of his reporter friend, the security guard offered Humph the use of his handkerchief to absorb the sweat on his brow.

"Do you guys follow the stock market?" Humph threw out the question to his friend before saying hello.

"Of course we do. Why?"

"I just invested for the first time. I went to a so-called brokerage on Broad Street. I think it used to be a drug store or something. It stunk. Of what, I don't know but if I had a favorite aunt I wouldn't let her even walk by the place. What I want to know is what happened today on Wall Street to a stock known as Ford Motor Company. I plunked down $10 and got $42 back. I have my doubts."

"Give me a few minutes," Gerry said. "Money is not my department."

It was 20 minutes before he returned.

"Here's what happened in trading of Ford shares today, hour by hour. Your stock, at the time of day you mentioned, fell by 1.2 percent. You should have lost money."

Humph stared at his young friend.

"That's the best news I've had all week."

The reporter called across the noisy newsroom to someone named Pat.

"Pat, I need to pick your brain!" he shouted over the clatter of typewriters, teletype machines and voices.

In newsrooms, the world seemed exciting, urgent, thought Humph. At his apartment, when he leaned out the window and looked down to the street, life seemed tawdry, tragic and petty somehow.

When Pat arrived, the young reporter introduced the older one. Pat leaned forward over Gerald who was between them, to shake hands. His grey hair had no visible part but it flopped to the right side with the gesture. "Like a mudslide down a cliff," Humph thought before wondering where the hell that image had come from.

When Pat retrieved his hand from Humph's, he used it to throw the hair back in place.

"How on earth did I make $42 so easily?," Humph asked. "I saw the stock ticker but it meant nothing to me. What the boy was writing on the big board didn't sink in either. And now you tell me I actually lost. Why did the broker tell me I made money?"

Pat's eyes were almost as grey as his hair. However, they twinkled at the question.

"I did so many stories on this impossibility years ago I'm amazed to learn that it is apparently easy to stumble into a good, old-fashioned bucket shop. They were outlawed, you know."

Humph didn't know.

"So why are they still open?"

"The simple answer is greed, both on the part of the so-called brokers and conmen who operate them and on the part of the general public, a public that has become profoundly smitten by the notion of making easy money. Do you know that millions of Americans now play the market?

"These joints are the only ones that will accept tiny investments, the only ones most people can afford. What the broker never tells a new investor is that he has entered a betting shop. After all, that might very well scare off a reasonable man who wouldn't ordinarily risk his meager savings on a horse or a baseball result. Better they think they're investing in America—a good deed in itself—while having their hand held by an experienced broker."

The old reporter's eyes lost their twinkle suddenly. He looked sadly at Humph and said:

"You were conned, lad."

Humph was more surprised at being called "lad" than learning that he'd been finessed.

"I'd wager," said Pat, "that they ignored the drop in price for the stock you plunked your money on and fabricated the happy outcome. They wanted you to keep investing, and with such as easy windfall, it's rather likely that either that day or a later day, you would have done just that. Gimme, gimme, gimme."

The old reporter said that on the day in question, he was dead certain the broker put his arm around Humph's shoulders—"if he could reach that high"—and waltzed him to the cashier's window.

"Ordinarily, you would give the cashier the slip you got from him when you placed your bet. That slip would bear the details of the investment, the amount, the stock in question, the margin and any other particulars. This time, however, your broker would have slipped a false slip, no pun intended, to the cashier. In other words, not the one that was prepared when you placed your investment. The cashier would know the game, of course, and would go along with the fiction that you were a winner and duly pay you your money if you'd chosen to sell your stock and claim the profit."

"If I've got this right," said the young reporter, "Pat is telling you that based on his investigations for past stories, the broker never sold your stock. Yes, he knew from the ticker that your Ford stock initially lost money but experience told him it would soon regain its original price and probably gain in value on the day. He paid your transaction out of the brokerage's own pocket and, later in the day, after you'd gone home happy, he'd have probably sold the stock at its higher price and easily recovered the money he lost making you happy."

"You're my best student, Gerald," said Pat. "You see," he said, turning to Humph, "these bucket shops are not real brokerages. They are betting shops, pure and simple. They reel you in, get you all exuberant with a winning stock, then talk you into larger bets. They happily lend you the money to double your bet and increase your odds of walking home with a fancy new dress for the missus. What you, the punter, probably don't know is that the margin they've offered you is a loan with interest. If you win, no problem. The broker takes his commission from your winnings but you still come out on top. Lose, however…"

Humph interrupted.

"When I lose," he asked, "don't I just lose the money I put down?"

Pat laughed.

"No, no, laddie."

He explained that yes, Humph would lose the amount he invested, but he would also owe the brokerage for the money he borrowed to up his investment. The margin.

"They charge you a healthy interest on that loan. You might as well go to a loan shark on the Bowery. You'd be out your investment, you'd be out the margin and the interest you had to pay. And you would no longer own the stock. The brokerage, in the case of a loss of value in the stock, automatically owns the stock and has the right to sell it."

Humph thought for several minutes, holding up his hand to the reporters to say, "Don't abandon me yet."

Pat didn't wait for Humph to deliberate to his heart's content.

"I think I can clarify the scam further. Allow me."

Humph nodded.

"I must add an important element to this scam. They didn't simply lend you the money to double your bet, for example. Had you returned to the shop, they would have offered you margin trading schemes. Leverage ratios could be as outrageous 100:1."

Seeing a blank look on Humph's face, he continued.

"The ratio I mentioned, 100:1, means that a deposit of $1 cash would allow you to supposedly buy $100 in stock. Inviting, yes?"

The truth, Pat said, was that the trades were illusory and not enacted in the real market.

"The broker also made no real margin loans. However, it did collect interest in cash from the client. You, lad, could easily imagine that you had been loaned a great sum of capital, in return for a small cash deposit and interest payment.

"When you agree to a certain margin, you agree to a set of totally arbitrary conditions intended only to further tilt possible outcomes in the brokerage's favor. These conditions would stipulate that your investment was valid only if the stock price didn't fall below or rise above a certain percentage. If it fell even momentarily to the limit of your margin, which was more than likely in a volatile market, you would instantly forfeit everything. You would lose your cash investment and be on the hook for the loan with interest."

Humph was beginning to feel sympathy for the spoiled rich kid in the Bronx. He could only imagine how a broker in the same shop would react when seeing the kid's tailored suit, the arrogant gaze, the condescending voice.

On his way home, Humph's mind was showered with thoughts about bucket shops and swindling the rich, a subject dear to his heart. Before he got off the trolley, those thoughts had given way to something dearer to his heart. Eve, kidnapped Eve, desperate Eve, dead Eve.

As he walked along Henry Street, he realized it wasn't tawdry. The people looked that way only because they had no choice, unlike the brokers of Wall Street or the scions of high-society millionaires. So what if his neighbors tried to deceive reality with a gawdy dress or cheap glitter.

People, Humph had decided long ago, have an infinite capacity to pretend. For most, life would be unbearable without that ability. A lonely middle-aged woman convinces herself she's only between lovers. A failing shopkeeper tells himself he's paying the price of honesty because he never jigged his scales to show that you bought a pound of pastrami instead of three-quarters. A young woman of average looks who works in the box office of the local cinema convinces herself a Hollywood producer will discover her. A stuttering actor in an amateur play believes he'll end up on Broadway. A gambler who wears his hat at a cocky angle believes he'll win big and never have to work again. Those pretensions, the ones everybody has, die a thousand deaths but never perish for good.

The dreams of people like young Frankie were different. They were brought up believing they could be whatever they wanted.

The day had convinced Humph that Ostenbruch was the key to everything. He decided to return to the brokerage the next day and try to intercept his secretary before she entered the office. He wanted to pick her brain for any other details about the broker and his doings outside the brokerage. Perhaps she would accept an offer to have tea with him during her lunch hour. She didn't look a coffee drinker. Humph had no idea what appearance would denote a coffee drinker. Stupid notion. Maybe he associated tea with gentle people. The secretary wouldn't harm a soul.

Just as he was falling asleep, there was a sharp knock at his door.

"A telegram for you, sir." A small, uniformed man handed Humph the message and stood waiting. He looked young, not much more than a boy. However he noticed that he had already mastered the appearance of stoic patience.

Humph ripped open the message at the same time as he reached across his big table where he'd tossed his pants. In mid-motion, he stopped and stood there, leaning over the table in his underwear, reading.

"Meet my place tomorrow. Have possibly important lead." It was from the Park Avenue pretender, Colin Lenester.

Humph looked up and saw the Western Union boy's expressionless face in the doorway. Humph picked up his pants and plunged his hand into the right pocket. All he found was a single dime. That would do. Stubbing his toe on the table yet again, he made his way to the door and handed over his tip.

"No reply, sir?" The boy explained that the sender had pre-paid a reply. The telegraph boy showed him a new message form.

Humph was paralyzed for a few seconds.

"Yes. Say 'Tomorrow noon your place.' Write it for me," Humph said. "I'm not well right now."

He wasn't ill. He just didn't know how to deal with hope in the face of the slim odds he faced in finding Eve.

Humph returned to his pants on the table and found enough coins to tip the boy generously.

After getting Humph's signature for the return message, the young man raised his right hand to his cap in thanks and headed back downstairs.

It was close to 4 a.m. before Humph embraced sleep. At 6:30 he was awakened by an accented woman's voice screaming, "Never you come back!"

"Never get married," Humph thought, sitting up on the edge of his bed. Occasionally, women still turned his head but their faces would sooner or later dissolve into Sunny's. He wondered whether he would ever find another woman. Sunny had been perfection. Her life ended before imperfections had a chance to make their relationship and earthly affair.

The next morning, Humph walked to Wall Street to give himself time to think of ways the fat broker might be in league with the likes of renowned mobster Owney Madden, known by many as the King of the West Side. What would Reginald Ostenbruch have to offer Madden? A few girls for the prostitution racket, yes, but guys like Madden had been harvesting bumper crops of their own for years. Any contribution the broker might make would be a drop in the bucket. There had to be some other connection.

When Humph arrived at the brokerage, the secretary signaled to him to wait outside. She appeared a few minutes later. To Humph's amazement, she blushed as he once again put a hand on her shoulder, drawing her closer so they wouldn't be overheard by passersby or anyone entering the brokerage.

"By the way," he whispered. "What's your name?"

"Edith," the secretary said. "Edith Fitzsimmons but you can call me Edith."

"Edith. I'm… well of course you know my name already."

"I came across something that might be of use to you, sir."

"If you're an Edith, I'm a Humph, not a sir."

She smiled and reached inside her purse. She pulled out a letter. Gently, Humph took it from her. It was more of a note than a letter. It read:

"Mr. Madden accedes to your request for a face-to-face powwow. A driver will be sent to your residence next Friday evening."

The letter was dated the previous month. The broker and the mobster, one known since his youth as The Killer, had met. Humph had heard about him as a cop and read about him in the papers.

Humph beamed at the secretary. He hugged her ever so briefly.

"Edith, would you have a few minutes, perhaps on your lunch break today, to join me for tea somewhere? Don't be alarmed. I'm not being forward. I would just like to pick your brain briefly."

The secretary regarded Humph for a moment, then her eyes dropped to her hands, which where clasped in front of her.

"Whatever for?" she finally asked. "I've told you everything I know, you know, in that letter I showed you."

"I don't really know, miss. I just thought that a few moments of reflection over a good cup of tea might trigger some memory."

Her eyes watched his closely as he spoke. At last, she said, "Yes. All right. If you think it might help. Mr. Ostenbruch is not in at the moment. I think I could probably join you in a few minutes." With that she turned abruptly and mounted the stairs to the main door.

When she returned, she was clutching a file folder.

"There's a tea salon a couple of blocks from here," she said. "On William Street."

Humph noticed her nervous, almost shy demeanor had been supplanted by something he couldn't pin down at first. By the time they had reached the tea salon, he decided that the secretary was displaying a sense of purpose or excitement. Did that have anything to do with the manila folder she carried?

At first glance, the tea salon appeared to be a pleasant refuge from the wheeling and dealing that dominated the nearby streets. The faded yellow of the patterned wallpaper spoke of a slower era, perhaps even a gentler one. The secretary led him quickly to a corner table, one that gave her a view out the window. Was it her table of preference? Why, Humph thought, would a lady like her feel the need to have her back to the wall like a Wild West poker cheat?

The question ceased to be of any import when he realized his bulk might present a challenge that the little chairs might not withstand. With two hands on the table, he sat as gently as a leaf floating to the ground. By continuing to hold the table and leaning forward, he made sure his weight was centered on the front edge of the chair.

Edith made no move to open the folder until after the tea arrived.

"I don't know what any of this means but the name Madden appears many times. It seems he and Mr. O have more than a passing acquaintance." She handed the folder to Humph.

Her tea was at drinking temperature by the time Humph looked up.

"You're a fast reader," she said.

"Yes, actually. I am. I trained myself to do so after discovering in my youth that there were more things I wanted to read than I had ever imagined."

"Was this at school?"

"No. At a public library, on Grand Street. I discovered it by accident when I was no more than 15. It became my home away from home, as they say."

Then Humph shut up. He'd said enough about himself to a stranger. The silence between him and the young woman lasted several minutes. She sipped her tea but kept her eyes on him. Her gaze was neutral. He was glad she asked no more questions.

Humph cleared his throat, excused himself and then betrayed his excitement.

"These papers. These documents..." Humph began tapping them forcefully with his forefinger.

The secretary waited and waited.

"Yes. Those papers?"

"They're not proof of anything. Those two are too careful to allow that but I'd wager my life that they are creating an empire of some sort. Look," he said, frantically leafing through the documents, "here. Read that," he said pointing to a paragraph.

Edith moved her teacup to the side of the table and took the document with both hands.

"It says, 'Everything's falling into place, Owney. Five more speaks have complied.' To which this Owney guy answered, 'Well done. I'd swear that if it wasn't for your moniker I'd believe you were Irish.' He goes on to add, 'That gives us 32 speaks. Eighteen more will be enough to get started. We'll eventually need a lot more but before getting them we need to get people to manage the places we have first.'"

The secretary looked at Humph. This time her eyes betrayed excitement with a touch of concern. For him?

"Here's what I'm thinking," Humph said. "They're building an empire of some kind. Look, there are now thousands and thousands of speaks in this city. They get busted by the hundreds every week but they're back up and running somewhere else before you can scratch an itch…" Humph stopped short of finishing the sentence.

"But what I didn't know was that someone is buying them up." He stared at the secretary. "But why?"

He downed half the contents of his teacup and answered his own question.

"Your boss and the gangster want—I read this term somewhere—they want a captive audience, if you know what I mean. If they own a million speaks, the patrons will be drinking only alcohol your guy and the Irish killer are peddling. For that to be truly profitable for them, they'll have to be the guys providing the bootleg hootch from its source."

"The what?" asked Edith.

"Oh, sorry. The alcohol. The illegal alcohol. The stuff people make here, most of which tastes worse than last week's fish fry. Some of it can kill you. And if you want to get rich on bootlegging, you import it from the polar bear, our neighbor to the north. Canada. It's all legal there."

For the first time that day, the secretary smiled.

"I've always heard that they are sensible people, those Canadians," she said.

A joke. Humph laughed loudly, stopping himself at the last second from reaching out to slap her on the back.

They sat in silence for a while. Finally Humph spoke.

"Oh my god. You've given me the evidence I need to go after them and, if the big guy up there is willing, to finally find my girl, my Eve."

Seeing the relief in Humph's eyes, Edith gingerly reached out to touch his hand.

"I don't know how to thank you," Humph said.

"Well, I think you can by walking me back to my office. Who knows whether I still have a job?"

Humph smiled and extended his hand.

"My lady."

When they got back to Broad Street, Humph said:

"Back to your desk before you're missed. Hurry, my dear." At the heavy door to the brokerage, she turned 45 degrees toward Humph and gave him a little wave of her hand.

The morning had started well, more than just well.

Buoyed, he looked for a deli to get some breakfast before heading uptown to Park Avenue. He had time to kill. The meeting was two hours away.

CHAPTER 7

HUMPH couldn't believe that walking on Park Avenue was already starting to feel like an every-day thing. He belonged, somehow, to the mythical mass of millionaires that lived there. Mythical, he had decided, because half of them were crooks, swindlers, embezzlers, con men, or fronts for nasty individuals. Colin Lenester, a newcomer to wealth, had nothing to feel ashamed of.

After Humph crossed the green courtyard, Lenester again met him at the door.

"Right on time, Humph," said Colin, pumping his hand. "I must tell you that since I left the employ of young Frankie's father I have made it a point to never ever be punctual. It's positively liberating."

Colin promptly led Humph to the Victorian easy chair he so loved on the last visit.

Once Humph was settled, Colin rubbed his hands together in excitement and announced:

"There have been developments since your last visit. I may have mentioned that I detest young Frankie's father but I would never have wished upon him what has just passed."

"I'm all ears," said Humph, sitting forward in his chair.

"As well as life insurance, racing horse insurance, madness insurance, name it, the old man had a product for every need or imagined need. His company was also actively involved in manufacturing and railroads, and motion pictures. Name it and he had a finger in the pie. I once overheard him say to a visiting executive of some sort that his company was growing even faster than America."

"Colin, Colin," interrupted Humph. "What's your news?"

"The old man has had a nervous breakdown. He doesn't even appear at the office anymore. The official word is gallstones. But I know as a fact that the man hasn't had a physical problem in his life. He doesn't even get colds. No, the truth is he is locked in his bedroom at his estate in Greenwich.

"It doesn't look like a prison. I have seen it. The room is huge. It's furnished like a king's chamber and floor to ceiling windows overlook grand gardens. But—and I know this from a servant I once commiserated with—the lock is big and solid."

"Colin, Colin, Colin..." Humph was growing increasingly exasperated. "What has happened that has anything to do with my investigation?"

"Aw, Humph, can't you let a man enjoy his moment of divine comeuppance?"

Humph allowed himself to smile and nod.

"Thank you, sir. Here's the story.

"The reason Frankie's dad has stepped to the other side of reality is that unbeknownst to almost everybody at the company, the third largest source of revenue for this giant of American capitalism was entirely illegal. Let me add here that the business is family owned. It's not public, so it was easy to keep secrets."

Colin was enjoying his performance, especially the fact that he'd put the big man on tenterhooks, no mean accomplishment, he figured, considering that Humph was very much a plodding sort. Humph was the type who had to be convinced beyond doubt before showing emotion.

"Frankie's papa was the majority shareholder in Montreal's biggest distillery. Yes, that's Montreal, Canada, home of the brave and the booze. When Prohibition shat on our country, Humph, Frankie's dad must have danced for joy. He held the key to wealth even he hadn't dreamed of."

Humph was floored, so much so that he couldn't immediately make any connections with his immediate case: the broker, the gangster and Eve.

"Care for a drink to help digest the news?" Humph waved off Colin's offer and began to pace.

"Can we go to the garden?"

Colin led the way. Humph walked around the courtyard for almost the entire length before settling on the bench he used before his first visit. Colin joined him. The two sat in silence. Colin heard the birds singing, one of the things he liked most about living there. Humph appeared not to hear anything beyond his own thoughts. Colin marveled at how still the big man sat.

Suddenly Humph's right arm darted to his left. His hand grabbed Colin's hand. For a moment, Colin froze, startled by the speed of the gesture. But seconds later he let out his breath when he realized Humph's hand wasn't crushing his.

"Young man," Humph said, his eyes fixing Colin's, "you have possibly unraveled a vast illegal empire."

The information was worth its weight in booze in

several possible ways. Humph figured he could pop into the Manhattan DA's office and ingratiate himself for life by revealing what Colin just told him. Or he could use it with the stockbroker or Owney Madden himself as leverage to get Eve out of their clutches. The latter course of action had two possible outcomes: the release of Eve or, for himself, cement shoes and a bath in the East River.

"Anything on paper to back up any of this?"

"Would you accept a file of receipts for train travel between New York and Montreal? By themselves, they don't prove anything beyond the fact that he was a frequent traveler to Montreal. Insurance men like him feel naked without dotted i's and crossed t's, or receipts for travel expenses and hotel accommodations. Did I mention the Ritz? It was his favorite."

Humph held his huge hands in front of him as if praying.

"And, by chance, Colin, are there any records of Customs receipts, bills of lading, inventory adjustments, purchase orders? If Frankie's dad is so persnickety about his business practices, is it possible he mixed illegal importations of hooch with his other business dealings?"

"Absolutely," said Colin, who quickly added that the man was not stupid. "One of his manufacturing companies regularly imported machine parts from Montreal. He had every legit reason to go there and have things shipped from there to New York."

Humph's eyes and Colin's met for at least a minute.

Colin spoke first.

"Are you going to ask me if I have access to those records?"

"As a matter of fact," said Humph, "I confess to even wondering whether you have them right here in your humble residence."

Colin smiled. By far, Humph was the smartest "big lug" he had ever met.

"I do, sir." Colin then called for his maid. In what

seemed like fluent Spanish, as Colin later explained, he asked her to fetch a brown box from under his bed.

"If you can't reach it," he said in English, "I'm sure I can think of someone with a long-enough reach."

It was Humph's turn to smile.

Five minutes later, her face reddish with exertion, the maid dragged in the box. It was heavy.

Colin thanked her with a quick hug and told her she could take the rest of the day off.

"Gracias, señor." She stepped quickly toward the main entrance, then stopped and turned.

"Y good day, Señor Humph."

Humph opened the box and saw a small mountain of documents.

"Before meeting me," he asked Colin, "what had you intended to do with these documents? What prompted you to collect them?"

Colin paused either because he needed to think or because he didn't think Humph would appreciate his answer. For a good minute, he appeared to fixate on his hands which were palms-up in his lap.

"I'm not exactly sure," Colin said. "When I went to work for Randall Overton and got to know the magnitude of his enterprises, I felt sure that there would be opportunities in abundance for me to make something of myself. In fact, my industriousness paid off in no time with a promotion to senior clerk. No one in my family back home in Philly ever made as much money as I was getting."

"Forty-one dollars a week, if I remember correctly," Humph said.

"Forty-three to be precise. That promotion only served to motivate me more. I worked extra hours as a matter of course. First in, last out sort of thing. On a number of occasions the big man, last in last out, found me alone in the office. I was sure he'd acknowledge me someday in gratitude to a loyal employee. Just a nod or 'Hello, young man.' But nothing, ever. To my knowledge, he never even looked at me, even when passing within feet of my desk."

Colin went on to say that a year passed and it was general knowledge that no one would be getting raises that year, even though one of the bookkeepers said the insurance division had been making record profits. Every day the papers ran a story telling their readers how the economy was booming like never before in its history. The bookkeeper's theory was that people now felt they could afford to buy insurance of all kinds, life, property, and even something called car insurance.

"As of this year," said Colin, "Ford has sold 15 million cars. Imagine that."

Colin then held up his hands and said, "I digress. Overton's stinginess in the face of landmark profits weighed on the whole office. I was still working hard and looking for ways to draw the attention of my superiors but all I got out of them was a pat on the back and statements to the effect they wished everyone applied themselves with my industry. 'Or even half of it,' he said, finding his own remark witty."

Colin went on to tell Humph that he was personally aware of several cases of financial desperation among his colleagues, tragedies that could be averted by nothing more than a fair wage.

"Forgive me, Humph, but I began to hate Randall Overton, pure and simple hatred. I had no idea how I'd ever get back at a scion of industry. Where do you start? Do you sneak into his office and put chewing gum on the floor under his desk, then hope that he tumbles over while scraping it off his shoes? The final straw came just over a year ago when one of my superiors asked me to bring a file to Mr. Overton's office. When I appeared at the door, he looked up, annoyed, and demanded, 'Who are you?' That was the camel's-back moment for me."

Humph, who had never held a job with an impressive title, empathized with the young man, despite the fact that he now led a life of luxury. Being a cop sounded good before you donned the uniform. There was camaraderie but there was little respect, from higher-ups at the precinct or the citizenry they were supposed to respect. There was one consolation, he thought. The abuse he got from criminals who found themselves suddenly wearing handcuffs was almost as good as praise from superiors. It's an upside-down world, he often thought. Perhaps that was why he always felt good when they not only seized booze from the speaks they busted but kept a lot of it for themselves. Humph was often proud of being the cop charged with securing it in the evidence locker. The guys would choose him because he was so tall he could reach the top shelf easily to hide the booze from view.

Humph was passionately opposed to the frequent bombings by anarchists in the city. That was going too far because it risked lives. In fact, even in his worst moments of resentment, Humph would never even resort to using his sledge-hammer fists unless physically threatened.

So, he figured, the kid, Colin, was going about revenge in the right way. Humph wanted to help the kid see the day when he proved he was the equal of a tyrant.

Colin gathered all the files.

"Tomorrow I'll arrange to have them delivered to you, Humph."

Humph was thrilled. He wouldn't be lonely in his flat for a long time. He wanted to memorize every move the rich bastard had made. Then he would begin planning the rescue of Eve. Who knows, maybe even Frankie, the big man's son, would be willing to contribute damning evidence or at least provide some leads.

"I'd better be heading home," Humph announced. "If I spend any more time on Park Avenue I'll get a fat head. From what I'm told, my noggin is big enough as it is."

For a small man, Colin had a strong handshake. It was probably just his show of appreciation, Humph thought as he stepped outside into a light rain. There wasn't a cloud in the sky when he started his day. As he walked toward the subway, he felt the rain was washing away the doubts he carried with him that morning. His investigation now sprouted tentacles reaching far and wide.

CHAPTER 8

THREE days later, Humph reached Frankie by phone.

At first Frankie seemed reluctant to talk about the financial drubbing he'd received by con men posing as stockbrokers. Had he admitted his loss to his father and been forgiven for disgracing the Overton name? Not likely, thought Humph.

"I'm trying to move on," Frankie finally said. After a long pause and with a whisper of shame in his voice, he said he'd begun a new career.

"A new career?" Humph asked.

"Well, my first career. The days of indolent playboy are over, Humph. I have plunged into the endeavors common to writers."

"Such as?"

"I have submitted a short piece about fraudulent brokers to none other than *True Manhattan Detective* magazine. Being a detective, you probably read it, do you not?"

"To be sure, I do, Frankie. When will the piece appear?"

"Still waiting for a response from the submissions editor. You know how it is."

Actually, Humph didn't but the subject of submitted manuscripts tugged at his own submerged urge to write someday.

"Hats off to you, young man."

Frankie seemed also to have abandoned his self-centered rudeness.

"Thank you, Humph." He quickly added that he had no intention of sitting on his backside while awaiting a reply.

"I'll be taking employment in a week in a half."

"Taking employment?" Humph asked. "Do you mean you're about to become someone's employee? Clock in at 8 and don't forget to bring a little lunch to eat at your desk? That kind of employment?"

Humph pinched himself to control his urge to be sarcastic. At first meeting, Frankie had come across as nothing less than a monstrously spoiled rich kid who thought he was god's gift to female playthings. Though Humph signed on to the case to investigate the supposed theft of the boy's money by a brokerage, he privately thought the boy deserved to lose the dough just on principle. But Frankie's check didn't bounce and Humph still hoped the case would be complicated enough to last a long while, thereby requiring additional payments.

"And what, if I may ask, is this new job?"

"I've been employed by a company called CBS. If you have a radio, Humph, you may have heard of it. Ultimately, I still wish to author novels. I accepted the job because it also involves fiction of sorts. I'll be joining a team of writers of radio adventures."

The pride was evident in his voice. Maybe the young man had actually turned a new leaf. He was standing his ground against his father who had ridiculed the idea of a son of his wasting his education as a compiler of words. If so, good for him, thought Humph.

"Do you have any news for me?" Frankie asked.

"I do in a way. Rather than news, I have questions."

"Ask away, Humph."

"Can we meet somewhere face to face? I have a reason for asking that."

"I guess, as long as it's before I start my job as a script writer." Humph had a feeling the young man was so happy to finally have a purpose in life that he repeated to himself every chance he got the fact that he had a job. Not only that but he had a job as a writer, the very ambition dear Papa had ridiculed.

"Let me explain. What I want to talk to you about is private and at the moment I'm calling you from one of the telephones at my local police precinct. The phone company reclaimed my phone. Some confusion about my bill. I didn't really pay much attention to their letter until they yanked the damn thing out. Anyway, my current locale is not very private."

"Sounds like a good scene for a detective radio show." Frankie laughed. It was the first time Humph had heard him laugh without sarcasm.

"Consider the scene yours. Now where do we meet? Do you ever come downtown?"

They agreed to meet in something called the Men's Bar of the Plaza Hotel on Fifth Avenue across from Central Park. Frankie said he was known there, or rather his father was. Humph had never been inside the hotel but he figured that since he could almost now be described as a habitué of Park Avenue he might conceivably fit in there. He made a mental note to reread *The Great Gatsby*. Lots of Plaza scenes if memory served.

Humph had never complained about his lot in life. He wasn't prone to envy either. But since taking on this case and being able to peek inside the world the other half lived in he sensed a twitch of discontent. Not for wealth. He had no idea of what he'd spend a fortune on. No, what he felt was an urge to make his world larger, to vanquish once and for all any sense of "us and them". This was America, after all. We're all equal.

By evening, he was already dismissing those musings as garbage. He'd be better off retaining his resentment of rich robbers if he hoped to crack the criminal cocoon that hid Eve.

Humph used the time before the Plaza meet to study the papers Colin handed over. He wanted to establish a link between the pillar of American industry and the booming bootlegging industry represented by one of Ireland's most despicable exports, mobster Owney Madden. If he could corral the slimy broker, Reginald Ostenbruch, he'd be a Triple Crown winner. Humph loved the fact that this year's Kentucky Derby winner was named Whiskery. Not for a moment did he think the word had anything to do with facial whiskers.

When he got through the papers, he was dizzy from the details. He was not a businessman. He wished Eve was with him again. Her mind meandered differently than his and had an uncanny ability to produce the answers he sought, about life, about women, about the cases he worked on, and about the damned decade he lived in. The Great War laid waste to Europe in the last decade. America, at least the cities, was under a different kind of attack. Mores and money seemed to be the battleground. Humph had long ago concluded he didn't know who the good guys and bad guys were.

CHAPTER 9

WHAT would Sunny have thought of all this?

Life was simpler when she was in his world, in his life not just in his head. After she died, she stayed there in that thing above his shoulders. He never liked the term brain because it wasn't something he could touch, clean, twist and straighten. Was the brain the same entity as a marriage between heaven and hell?

In time, the debate ended. She was just something hovering simultaneously above and within him. She was as beautiful as ever. As peaceful as ever with her smile. But while he could feel her he couldn't touch her. She was just there, like a tour guide for his life. Turn left at the next block, cross to the other side of the street, talk to her but don't talk to him, stop being sad, you have no reason to be, watch out! get off the road, now there is a woman for you,

Humph, see, the one under the light standard, she is lost, come on Humph, go over, say hi and take her where she wants to go.

Sunny, the spirit, was never wrong. But the years went by and because she was never wrong Humph never looked, seriously looked, at another woman. He was never sure that was true but it was only after Sunny started to become less distinct in his thoughts, his memories, his neutral moments as he sat on a park bench, or when he lay in bed, too tired to construct thoughts, let alone open the door to feelings. Those were his weakest moments. Sunny would appear, neutral, calm. She always filled the void, like a Buddha statue floating inches above a smiling corpse.

Where the hell was her daughter, their daughter? Eve, for Christ's sake, come to your mother!

But she never appeared in his dreams with Sunny.

One night, too tired to think about those papers, he drank his fill. It was Canadian whiskey purchased at a speak nearby. It was owned by a petty crook Humph knew from his copper days. They never pinned anything serious on him, though the odds were good that he was a key middleman. What Humph most remembered was that he was convivial at the moment he was busted, then again when he was arraigned, and when he stepped out of the hoosegow a few weeks later he was still smiling. He could be useful in the future, Humph thought. As part of his strategy, Humph maintained a friendly contact with him as a bootlegger. Nothing unusual for a cop in the later days of Prohibition.

When Humph sobered up the next day, instinct told him to visit the convivial bootlegger again.

The club he ran was literally a hole in the wall. Humph's shoulders were almost too wide to let him pass inside without turning sideways and shuffling his way in. The sign out front read, "One Way Street." Was that ominous or welcoming? He decided it meant something like "Point of no return." New Yorkers had grown to love the feeling of doing something illegal when they settled in for an evening's drinking.

The bootlegger, in his role as barkeep, greeted Humph with the offer of a drink on the house. Although it was painful to do, Humph shook his head No.

Humph grilled him about speaks that serve girls as well as booze. However, he soon realized he was striking out.

"You're talking about the big boys, Humph. I figured a long time ago that I'll live longer if their names never cross my lips." Humph then said, "Madden?" and left the name hanging. The barkeep could stare as long as Humph.

"One last question," Humph said. "Do you know of a guy named Ostenbruch, Reginald Ostenbruch?"

"I know the name but not the man," said the barkeep.

At least that was something, one more indication that the broker was up to his armpits in bootleg booze.

Two mornings later, on the day of the meet at The Plaza, Humph took special care with his straight razor. He cursed that he was still breaking in a new badger hair shaving brush. His impatience to get answers from Frankie made the shave last an eternity. When he was done, he looked in the mirror and saw his black hair was still in full anarchy from a restless night's sleep. He didn't use it every day but today Brilliantine was in order. He hoped it wasn't a windy day because it didn't provide much hold. Unlike most men, Humph wore no moustache, let alone the dominant handlebar stash. He also rarely wore a hat. He figured he was tall enough without a bowler perched on top.

On his way to the Plaza, he stopped for a shoeshine. If Sunny had been with him, he would have asked if he was Plaza-ready.

Walking through the lobby of the hotel made him feel like Colin Lenester must have felt on his first day as a tenant in a luxury building on Park Avenue. Definitely pleasurable but not enough to wash off the feeling of being an imposter.

He soon found the bar Frankie had chosen. He stepped inside and spotted Frankie at a table with his back to the entrance. Humph would obviously be seated across from him, facing the entrance. Did Frankie not relish being seen with him?

Frankie immediately extended his hand but didn't stand to shake Humph's. Maybe he was hungover, Humph thought. After the pleasantries were done with, Humph concluded the young man wasn't hungover. But he was anxious.

A waiter appeared immediately. Frankie order two cups of their best afternoon tea.

Humph knew the routine from having surveilled bars suspected of violating the Prohibition laws. The bar had no bottles on display but waiters routinely entered a door marked "Personnel Only" and reappeared with cups of fine bone china and bottles of water and, he imagined, soda. Humph never mixed his drinks.

Without taking a sip, Humph began:

"What bedevils me, Frankie, is not knowing how the esteemed broker, Mr. Reginald Ostenbruch, knew you would be appearing at what was for someone of his position in the financial world a disreputable bucket shop on Broad Street. How was he there to relieve you of $10,000? It's as if he was expecting you. How could that be? I don't buy coincidence."

Frankie looked pained.

"I should have told you this before. Ostenbruch knows my father. But at first I didn't make any kind of connection between what happened to me and that fact. My father knows everyone in that world. I thought I'd simply been naïve and walked into the wrong kind of brokerage. I was too much in a hurry to show my father I could succeed without him and his damn empire."

Humph let Frankie cool off. For well-bred Frankie, it had been an outburst. When Frankie finally spoke, his Overton upbringing surfaced.

"My dear father is a faux aristocrat, through and through. He would rather be knighted by the king of England, Georgie boy or whatever his name is, than remain a mere American captain of industry."

Humph let the young man catch his breath.

"That, Humph, my commoner friend, is why I wish to be a mere writer."

For the first time, Humph believed him. His ambition was real and it had nothing to do with money.

"Thank you for your frankness, Frankie. Who knows, maybe we can get to the bottom of this case after all." When he took on the case he had no hope whatsoever of getting Frankie's money back.

Humph wanted to know if Frankie truly thought his father would set him up for a 10-grand humiliation out of spite or was the whole affair more complicated.

"When you put it that way, Humph, it's a bit much. It's hard to believe my father would even bother to give me that kind of slap in the face. He doesn't have the time of day for me."

"OK, Frankie, that's a starting point for us. Do you have any idea about the connection between Ostenbruch and your father? In my opinion, after two meetings, Ostenbruch is not the kind of man anyone would truly want to be friends with."

Frankie shrugged his shoulders.

"Businessmen are happy to do business with any variety of snake," Frankie said. "Friendship never enters into it."

After a moment he summoned the waiter. He had been lurking. Was it because Frankie's dad was that valued by the Plaza, or was it in anticipation of a good tip?

"Same again, sir?"

Frankie barely nodded.

Humph broke a lingering silence by asking if Frankie knew anything about his dad's visits to Montreal.

"Not much. He took me there once when I was around

10 years old. I'm not sure why because most of my time there was spent with a nanny. I remember a few years later my mother demanding to accompany him on his next trip to Montreal. It turned into the only fight I ever witnessed between them. My mother was truly angry. I never saw her like that before nor after. I never figured out why she was insisting so much but it didn't make any difference. My father demanded that she silence herself. That's how he put it. 'Silence yourself!' I guess I remember that because he said it so loudly. It was rare that he ever raised his voice. As I got old enough to understand a little about adults, I began to theorize that my father had a woman in Montreal. I now wonder whether my mother suspected the same thing and that's why they fought that day.

"By the way, Humph, I remember that we stayed at a grand hotel with the name 'Ritz' in it. It was apparently quite new and my father dragged me throughout the building, the lobby, the bars, the restaurants, the kitchens. I learned from my mother years later that my father had wanted to be among the first investors in the hotel. I think she said the existing original investors turned him down. I can only imagine how livid that rejection would make him."

"Yet," said Humph, "you think he still stays there, at the Ritz, when he visits?"

"To the best of my knowledge."

Humph was now more curious than ever to piece together Randall Overton's life in his home away from home. To link the industrialist to bootlegging in a way that would get him taken to court in New York would take a lot of gumshoe sweat. He made a note to visit New York's Ritz-Carlton.

Humph returned his thoughts to Frankie and the bucket shop humiliation.

"Did you father know beforehand that you were planning on investing money?"

"He certainly did. He called me a fool. Since I knew nothing about investing in the stock market, I ignored the insult, which was by no means the first I'd received from Dear Papa. I asked him to tell me where to go to begin. That's how I ended up where I did. When I left his place, I asked him to wish me luck. He didn't reply."

The next piece of the puzzle, according to Humph's always ordered mind, was figuring out why the big-shot broker, Reginald Ostenbruch, got involved in a family dispute between father and son. Was he doing the industrialist a favor by ripping off his son, or was he bloodying the industrialist's nose for some reason?

Humph was sure there was no point at the moment in seeking clarification again from Ostenbruch. It would be some time before he was invited back to enjoy the downtown paradise of Gramercy Park.

Frankie clearly didn't know the answers to those questions. Humph rose from his chair and reached out to shake Frankie's hand.

"Good luck with your writing."

That drew an appreciative smile from the seemingly reformed young man.

CHAPTER 10

HUMPH decided his next stop would be on Park Avenue. On the way to Colin's building, he made a point of walking to Park via 46th Street when he left the Plaza in order to pass by the Ritz-Carlton.

Humph enjoyed investigating. It beat doing the Sunday crossword, which had first appeared in the *New York World* just over 10 years earlier and quickly became a passion for New Yorkers. His friend at the paper, Gerald Franklin, however, said he considered them a tad frivolous. Regardless, gumshoe work had it beat.

As he passed the hotel, he wondered whether doormen at hotels like that accepted bribes as easily as those at humbler hotels.

Once again, Colin was home. When Humph said he was pleased to find him there, Colin smiled his easy smile and reminded Humph that he was now a man of leisure despite his youth.

Humph sat and in a sonorous voice announced the reason for his visit:

"The Ritz."

"Aha, the Ritz!" Colin rolled the "r" in Ritz. "What about it?"

"Your former boss, Sir Randall..."

Colin interrupted.

"Sir Randall? Did he manage to buy a knighthood? I didn't know they were for sale."

Humph laughed.

"I'm trying to find a link between Overton and illegal importation of alcohol from Montreal, as well as a link between the bastard broker Ostenbruch and speakeasies in general, and of course anything linking either of them to Madden. Overton and Ostenbruch. Are they friends or foes?"

"I am quite sober, Humph, but I fail to see any connection between your questions and the R-R-R-Ritz."

Humph asked if he spoke Spanish.

"Yes. I wanted to converse with my lovely maid. I thought her presence here would be preferable to my presence in a language school. A more efficient use of time and such. Besides, as an idle man, mastering vocal acrobatics has killed a lot of time."

Humph smile again and raised his hand to make sure Colin would now seriously listen to what he was saying.

"Did your study of Overton's Montreal documents ever suggest the importation of alcohol, beyond the fact that he was the biggest shareholder in a Montreal distillery? Did the name Ostenbruch ever appear in those documents? Also, did your study of them ever suggest there was an investment in the Montreal Ritz-Carleton Hotel, and finally— are you ready?— a relationship with a young lady of the Montreal night, or any other lady for that matter?"

"I wasn't looking for any of those things. I'd have to study those documents all over again. For the moment, all I can say concerns the things I speculated about over time."

Humph assured him the wait was no problem. He was after solid evidence no matter how long it took to accumulate. Colin's response was to call for his maid in Spanish. Her name was Rebecca. An "r" to roll for Humph's benefit.

"No kidding, Humph. She says she doesn't recognize her name unless I roll the 'r'."

When Rebecca arrived, she said "Señor Humph" and gave a hint of a curtsey. Colin asked for two bourbons.

They didn't speak until the drinks arrived.

"To be honest, Humph, I must try to restrain myself. I would love to see Overton's world come crashing down for the simple reason that he's a self-bloated prick. The data I gave you is just that, data. I collected it but I didn't truly analyze it. I was just happy having it. I suspected it could be useful someday but I didn't know how.

"So, what suspicions did this information give birth to?" Humph was beginning to suspect that Colin's mind worked much like his own. No rush to judgment. No premature conclusions.

"Let me think on this for a while, Humph. I'd hate to erroneously impugn the reputation of New York society's golden boy but now that I'm rich, idle and rather bored, I find escape in indulging things of a conspiratorial nature."

Humph was halfway through his drink before Colin emerged from his thoughts.

What Colin proposed was vastly more intriguing than Humph's theories. Humph had been toying with the idea that Overton wanted to embrace the 18th Amendment in an unthinkable way for someone in his position. He wanted to become an invisible bootlegger of fine Canadian whisky. He wanted to dominate the city's tens of thousands of speakeasies as an exclusive supplier. Humph could easily imagine Overton believing himself to be so respected by all and sundry that no one would suspect for even a moment that he was engaged in an illegal enterprise. His trips to Montreal were obviously required to tend to his other business interests. He had receipts galore, Colin had said. The only element that Humph could not insert into the scenario was the broker. He knew Overton and Ostenbruch would know each other but why would the broker want to hurt and humiliate Overton's son?

While waiting for Colin to surface, Humph absentmindedly watched Rebecca quietly dust shelves of books and knickknacks. Were those books ones Colin had read or did he, like so many rich people, simply buy a library that would make him look intellectual or artistic? His eyes returned to Rebecca. She was graceful, he thought. A moment later, he revised the adjective: she was sexy. Damn bourbon, he thought as Colin began to speak.

"Humph, the scenario that tickles my sense of the conspiratorial the most is this. I'll just say it straight out.

"My theory, supported by little or no proof, is that Overton is dreaming big and dreaming bad. Like everyone, from pauper to president, he hates boredom and routine. His grand plan, Humph, is to become the bootleg king of New York. Furthermore, and this I say without any foundation, he wants to become the king of the speaks. He has the resources to buy out hundreds of them right now. My thought is that should he do that, he would deny other speaks access to his Montreal imports. His speaks would be meant for people with taste.

"I'm thinking this just because the man's a snob with an affected English accent. He would tell himself something like that, namely, 'I may be breaking an absurd law but I am doing it to bring refinement and good taste to the speakeasy industry.' Hogwash, of course, but I swear, Humph, that he's capable of that degree of illusion."

Humph put his glass on the floor, a gesture that sent Rebecca hurrying over to pick it up, and quietly applauded Colin in slow motion.

"Continue," Humph said.

"This is where the drama heats up, Humph."

Rebecca was trying to hand the glass back to Señor Humph but his eyes were fixed on Colin. Rebecca gave up. She retreated and returned with another glass of bourbon. Colin had paused, wanting to present his conspiracy's conclusion with absolute clarity.

"The link," he announced, "between Overton and the broker is this. Remember, the broker and that scary Irish gangster, are working together to dominate the speak scene in the city. The last thing they would want would be someone like Overton trying to do the same thing. The broker arranged to humiliate Frankie to wake Overton up to the dangers of messing with him and Owney Madden. Overton must have told Ostenbruch at some point that his wayward son wanted to become an investor. Ostenbruch told him to send Frankie to his place, where he'd be taken be in good hands."

Humph was staring at Colin so hard his eyes hurt.

"How did Ostenbruch know exactly when the kid would show up? He didn't but he gambled on the fact that the industrialist would have recommended him to Frankie. Ostenbruch had seen a family photo of Frankie and would have alerted the brokerage staff."

Now it was Humph's turn to ask for time to think. It turned out that he didn't really need it.

"Why did they kidnap Eve?"

Colin looked at Humph and felt his pain.

"I don't know. What if her kidnapping had nothing to do with any battle between Overton and the broker? I certainly can't imagine a connection. That would leave only one possibility. The broker and the gangster run a whole bunch of speaks and they also control a whole bunch of prostitutes. For some of their classier speaks, they want entertainment to be on the menu. Your girl was in burlesque. She dances and sings. And, if I remember correctly, she strips. If I put myself in Madden's skin, I would see dollar signs if I looked at your girl. I'm guessing she's being held at one of his places, doing what he wants her to do, and having no way of escaping. Girls like her are grabbed off the streets every day, Humph. I hate to say it but that's my guess."

Humph knew he was right. At least he now had a map of an ugly world. He had a starting point.

Humph stood and offered Colin his hand.

Colin rose and looked up to Humph's eyes.

"All sounds crazy, doesn't it?"

"Crazy, yes," Humph replied. "But that's what makes it sound real. Can't explain it but we're living in a crazy age."

"That we are," replied Colin, half turning and slowly swinging his arm across the expanse of his Park Avenue palace, the books, the artwork, the cabinet of ornate china, the marble fireplace, the little antique end tables, the hand-woven carpets.

"I'd be half-embarrassed, too. Good day, my friend."

CHAPTER 11

WHEN Humph awoke the next morning, he was depressed. That surprised him. Yesterday, as he listened to Colin's speculations, he felt sure he had a starting point for his investigation. Investigations in the plural to be accurate. He needed to solve the defrauding of Frankie and he needed to find Eve. Until yesterday he had no clue as to Eve's possible fate. On his way home he lectured himself. He mustn't let himself abandon Frankie and concentrate exclusively on Eve.

Humph didn't even want to get dressed. He sat at his scarred table in his underwear and waited for his coffee to be ready. After just one sip, he decided something that went against his nature. He wanted help, at least for today. The weight of his worry about Eve—was she even alive?—sometimes shut down his mind. He would go to the old precinct and find out what shift his buddy Charles Duffy was working. His plan after finishing coffee Number 2 was to trek to Duffy's place and convince him to book off sick. Duffy had gone out of his way during and after the precinct's stationhouse booze-up to help Humph. He had provided the connection between the gangster and the broker for starters. Humph would play on Duffy's cop instincts again, even if he had to spend the day drinking.

Duffy lived on the Bowery, just above Grand. The place was a step up from the street's many flophouses but it was clearly not a place where a cop on the take would live. Humph had always wondered how profitable Duffy's 18th Amendment workaround operations were. Maybe his Irish wits were too sharp to allow himself to betray his real income.

Humph had to bang repeatedly on Duffy's door before the constable's weary face appeared. As a peace offering, Humph handed him a loaf of the new pre-sliced bread and a donut. Humph brought the offerings on the assumption that Duffy would be hungover and in need of easy-to-swallow food.

"You big oaf, what the fuck would you be wantin' at this hour?" Duffy grabbed the donut before stepping back to let Humph enter.

Duffy ate the donut in silence after waving Humph to a chair. He took his good old time licking his fingers when the treat was gone. He was making Humph pay for the morning intrusion. Humph held back a chuckle.

Finally, Duffy pulled on a pair of pants and left the flat. "The shit shed calls."

As modern as the decade appeared, Humph thought, there were still hundreds if not thousands of tenements that offered only outhouses in backyards and alleyways.

When Duffy returned he was cursing the neighbors he had to wait behind before relieving myself.

"There was a woman, a woman not worth a second look to start with, who had four wee ones in tow. I begged her to let me step in front of her and her brood, but no. You'd almost think she had a hate on for our species."

However, the opportunity to gripe clearly was picking up his spirits.

"OK, Humph. Out with it."

Humph wasn't sure where to start.

"You remember what we talked about last time?"

"Surely I do. A tragic thing that's befallen your young Eve."

"Well, Duffy, there's been no word and I need your wisdom to tell me where to start looking. I've gotten some new information about the broker and a connection with Owney Madden. I'm sure the broker won't agree to see me again and I can't very well walk up to Madden and demand to know where Eve is."

Humph tried his best to summarize the documents Colin had assembled and, even more difficult, to present Colin's articulate speculations.

"I am in possession of those documents about the Montreal interests of my client's father. I have brought them with me."

"Humph, to be honest with ya, I doubt I could make head nor tail of them. I'll accept you friend's conclusions."

Humph then went on to explain the most painful part of Colin's conjectures.

"Basically, it sounds possible, if not likely that our gangster friend and the bastard broker are trying to set up a speakeasy empire. Our gangster friend wants to put many of his hundreds of prostitutes to work in his speaks. They would be like no other speaks. They would be… how to put it…full-service speaks. Booze and ladies of the night, a finger snap away. My friend on Park Av. went on to say it was very likely that the mobster and the broker were also going to turn some of their speaks into mini-burlesque houses. That would be their way of competing with the likes of uptown palaces like the Cotton Club that offered headline musicians.

"Makes sense. Makes sense, lad," said Duffy. He had been listening intently, which Humph appreciated. But his hands were also twitching.

"The end point, Duffy, is that Eve was a burlesque performer and stripper. She's more than comely. What if it turns out that Madden's gang has done the kidnapping and is holding her against her will in some bug-infested hole awaiting an assignment in one of their newly acquired speaks?"

"Got ya, got ya, lad. Hold the reins while I get mobile."

He returned from his bedroom fully dressed as a cop.

"Some authority might help us out on our interrogations today."

"Sit," Humph ordered. "What's your plan? I don't intend to go Willy-nilly everywhere. I can do that without your help."

While Duffy sat on his sofa leaning forward with elbows on knees and massaging his temples, Humph summarized what Colin had conjectured. When he finished, he asked simply:

"What is the shortest route to Eve and her kidnappers?"

The veteran cop kept his elbows on his knees while tilting his head up to look directly at Humph. The furrowed brow appeared to cause him even more pain.

"To be blunt about it, Humph, they, whoever they are, either took Eve to kill her for some slight we don't know about, or they have some use for her. Let's pray that it's the latter. If it is the latter, based on what your Park Avenue buddy said about everybody wanting to dive into the big-time speakeasy business, we have to start sticking our noses into Owney Madden's collection of speaks. I know, Humph, that you want to police your own imbibing but when duty calls, it calls. I would behoove us—

is that a real word?—to wet our palates repeatedly to see everything and everyone on display in the speaks with entertainment and girls to top up your drinks just right, if you take my meaning. Who knows, we might just spot Eve without having to ask a million people questions. If we have to interrogate, we'll pose as a couple of gents looking for a good-time gal they used to know."

Humph was surprised at how quickly Duffy's mind had recovered from the night before. Did he think more clearly hungover? That would indeed be a blessing, thought Humph, remembering doing battle with many a booze-induced fog of his own.

"And, no, Humph," Duffy said, not waiting for Humph's agreement on his strategy. "There's no point investigating that rich fella, the industrialist guy who may be setting up a hooch-line from Montreal. That wouldn't help us with Eve. She's more important right now than the fucking 18th Amendment."

For the price of a donut and a loaf of sliced bread, Duffy had put Humph on track. Humph felt hope, a little at least, which was a lot more than he felt last night.

Duffy was a bulldog. It was a characteristic Humph had often been credited with when he was on the force. The difference between them was that Duffy was also a bulldog in building his own scams with recovered goods, from booze to jewelry. Unlike Humph, Duffy appeared to feel no shame at all on the occasions when the sergeant asked him to explain where he got this, or how such and such was no longer in the evidence lockup. Duffy could deadpan with the best of them.

Humph even asked Duffy about that talent. Again, without the slightest embarrassment, he answered:

"I perfected it years ago when I found myself juggling two or three girlfriends at the same time. A suspicious species birds are."

Duffy disappeared momentarily and came back with his uniform buttoned up and his hair combed. Without a word he went out the door of the apartment and paused on the stairs only when he realized Humph wasn't on his heels. When Humph appeared, he was tearing off a big bite of white bread. He had two slices of the stuff in his hand.

"A starving man will eat anything," Humph said, closing the door behind him.

When his mouth was no longer full, he tapped Duffy on the shoulder.

"This is too damned early in the day to start hitting up the speaks."

"Agree. But there's somewhere else I want to go first."

They walked briskly down Bowery to Broome Street and took it to Center Street and police headquarters.

"There's a woman I want you to meet," said Duffy, breaking a long silence. "She's the head of the police matrons. As you might figure, Humph, she has a soft spot for her sex."

"Matrons? Matrons? Who the hell are they?"

"Humph, are you telling me you never had to deal with a matron assigned to the precinct to look over your shoulder when you hauled in a bunch of women? Too busy looking at the free flesh, right, lad?"

Suddenly he remembered. The first time he saw a matron at the precinct was when a male arresting officer was on the verge of tossing his collar back on the street in return for what he called "compensation" to be paid at a later date, or, if the lady preferred, she could be processed now with the other ladies of the night..

The desk sergeant paid no attention to the suggestion of sexual compensation. He'd seen just about everything from both criminals and his own cops. One of the benefits of cynicism is that you're never surprised, never disappointed. Result: there was nothing worth getting steamed up about. Good for the heart, thought Humph. Humph wasn't even close to being a cynic, but the lid on his emotions was as tight as the damn hat he had to wear as a constable.

He remembered being told later that the matrons were a kind of policewoman. In fact that was their rank. They were appointed to precincts about 15 years before to monitor how cops, the male ones, treated women in custody. Only now did Humph remember a drunken detective telling him one night how the NYPD salary, even for detectives, was shite but the free girlies made up for it. The matrons were there to remove the practice. Humph never gave it another thought since he had never for a second considered using his badge as a carte blanche for coupling.

Duffy led Humph to a door that read Chief of Woman's Division of the NYPD.

As Duffy knocked on the door, he turned to tell Humph he should address her as detective.

"You're kidding," Humph whispered.

"No sir. They're all full-fledged cops now."

The woman behind the desk didn't look stern despite the epaulettes that shouted captain. For some reason, Humph expected someone who looked like a broad-shouldered guard able to keep the peace at the city's nastiest edifice known as The Tombs. Being incarcerated there was hell, so was working there. Just the previous year, three inmates somehow got guns and tried to escape. They failed but three prison workers died, including the warden.

The captain clearly knew Duffy. He got a quick nod from her. As for Humph, she stared at him long enough to be impolite.

"Who's he?" she finally asked Duffy.

"A man too honorable to have remained among us saints in blue, captain. He was one of us but now works as a private investigator. He was a good lad, Ma'am."

The captain instructed Humph to sit.

"I'm Captain Connolly in case Duffy failed to inform you. I'm seeing you only because your reprobate companion once did me a favor. He disarmed a working girl who smiled her way into getting an officer to let down his guard while she was being held at the precinct for questioning. She grabbed his gun and for some reason pointed at me. Stupid girl didn't know I was there for her protection."

"May I ask what happened?" asked Humph.

"A constable laughed and slapped her arse. Hard. She spun around, the gun went off, and the desk sergeant's bloody head ka-thunked onto the counter he presided over. It took only seconds for police stupidity to take its toll."

Duffy squirmed in his seat. Humph, on the other hand, instinctively felt he'd met a brother, or rather, a sister.

Duffy didn't want any more personal assessments going on. He told the captain in simple, straight-forward terms what had happened, namely "what was surely a kidnapping of a young woman who came from a family of vaudeville performers and strippers and had no bad habits and was closely and loyally tied to her step-father, ex-officer Humph, here, seated to my right." Duffy had let the statement run on the way he kept his notebook. Humph once bet him that he couldn't find a single period in the entire thing. Humph won.

Duffy wasn't quite finished summarizing:

"She may have done something to enervate a certain well-established Wall Street broker who was trying to use her for sexual purposes. Humph and I investigated her disappearance immediately and could only conclude that she had been abducted in broad daylight. Inquiries made at both the office and home of said broker big shot proved fruitless. He was impenetrable if I may use such a word."

"You Irish do love your words, don't you?"

To Humph's relief, the captain cracked a smile.

"I can deal with her," he thought.

Humph then stepped in to state the rest of the facts that he thought substantiated his suspicions about her having been nabbed to serve as a stripper-prostitute-slave in one of Owney Madden's establishments.

"Madden and the broker are partners, Captain. And they both want to create a speakeasy empire. They're already well on their way to doing so. I'd venture a guess that they only need a dozen or more to control most of the city's drinking."

The captain regarded Humph for a minute then turned her chair to face the wall to her left. The wall was painted black. Humph had never seen a black wall in the department. Was it her invisible blackboard for theories? He looked for chalk but found none.

Finally, she turned to face the two men again.

"What do you want from me?"

"I want my girl back, Captain. I love her and she his my only living memory of a woman I loved more than I thought possible."

Humph said it with such unabashed sincerity that, at the same moment that the embarrassed Duffy covered his face with his hands, the captain's eyes softened.

"Has this girl ever been arrested? Has she ever been in jail?"

Humph rose and shook his big head slowly. Later, the captain was to tell Duffy that,

"The expression on the big guy's face was so full of pain I wanted to hug him and tell him I'd do anything to get his girl back." Then after a moment she added: "That's the kind of cop we need. How did we let him go?"

Duffy was touched by her response but later on he said he still couldn't countenance the idea of more women cops.

"They just don't get it. We're dealing with dogs, dirty mean dogs all the time."

Humph explained to the captain that he and Duffy were planning on hitting all the speaks they thought were owned by Madden, and maybe the broker as well, one by one in an attempt to find Eve and gather evidence against the broker and Madden.

The captain interrupted.

"You say your girl's name is Eve? She wouldn't by chance be ambivalent about her sexuality would she?"

Humph was thrown aback.

"What does that even mean?" he said.

"It's not what the Good Lord quite intended, Humphrey, but some women prefer the company of women."

"Why on earth are you asking that? What could that possibly have to do with her kidnapping?"

"These are complicated times, Humphrey."

"Humph! Humph! Call me Humph!" There was annoyance in his voice but the use of Humphrey wasn't the reason.

"Let me explain," the captain said. Mollifying ruffled feathers wasn't usually in her repertoire but she was still touched by Humph's sincerity.

"Just about a year ago, my girls and I raided a gay and lesbian tearoom, called Eve's Hangout, in Greenwich Village and arrested its proprietor. Her name was, as you might guess, Eve something. I have to ask if that was possibly your Eve?"

"God no. My girl's gotta boyfriend. I think he's a rather useless layabout but it's far from me to judge what's in a girl's heart."

"Just checking. Just checking," said the captain quietly.

She had a natural authority. She didn't have to bellow like many senior officers did. They acted like they were in the military. They made you feel stupid and at night you heard yourself saying, "Why should I help a self-important prick like that?" Humph, like Duffy, became expert at silent sabotage. The officers with big yaps never got the results they wanted and there was always convenient evidence to demonstrate that they hadn't known what the hell they were yelling about.

The captain was clearly different.

"My girls are the best means of attack, not you two."

"Your girls?" asked Humph.

"Yes. Maybe you don't know but in a rare attack of wisdom, the NYPD decided about 30 or so years ago that women provided the best means doing undercover work, of infiltrating gangs, prostitution rings, gambling, back-alley abortionist operations, in fact, any place where men are so stupid as to think that women are good for sex but somehow did not possess eyes and ears, the tools of a good copper. We were so good at it that they allowed us the title of matrons. By the early years of this century, we were full-fledged women in blue. Cops, just like you two. Some of us are even detectives, a rank neither of you has reached."

"Point taken, captain," said Humph, jumping in before Duffy had a chance to splutter. "So the men who raided Eve's Salon were in fact your girls, your officers?"

"Yes, sir. And we can use them to infiltrate the speaks one by one. Girls talk to girls, you know. They say things they'd never say to the likes of you two."

After a pause, during which the captain and Humph maintained an appreciative regard, Duffy asked:

"Do these ladies, these officers, wear pants?"

The captain ignored him.

"I'll get back to you, Humph. In short order, I hope. Now I have to toss you out. Another appointment awaits outside my office."

CHAPTER 12

AFTER the meeting with the women's division captain, Duffy said his hangover still needed more food. They entered the first diner they found. Duffy ordered a pork chop and mashed potatoes, heavy on the gravy. Humph settled for a coffee and peach pie.

As they ate, they decided to go to a speak or two immediately, ones they figured Madden owned.

"The detective won't have had time to send her girls out," Duffy said.

Humph didn't really see the point in jumping the gun. Let the ladies do the leg work for them. Then a sideways glance at Duffy's Irish-grey complexion gave sense to Duffy's suggestion. He needed a damned drink.

"Where do you want to go?" Humph asked.

"There's a bar in the Bronx I once busted back when we cops were doing the Prohibition policing."

"The captain said her people will do the investigating," Humph interrupted.

"A reconnaissance by a thirsty damn Irishman, that's all this'll be."

Federal agents did the policing now. New York courts had been inundated with thousands of Prohibition cases and ended up trying to fine hundreds of violators at the same time to clear the backlog. There were often more defendants than would fit in a court room.

In the words of one justice, the paralysis of the courts had become "beyond ridiculous". Rather than hear individual cases, which would take time and non-existent manpower, offenders were often simply fined a buck and let go.

At the same time, the NYPD had made a mockery of speakeasy enforcement. For the cops, who barely earned $2,000 a year, enforcement meant untold opportunities for payoffs from bar and club owners and gave them an open invitation to seize immense quantities of hooch, which became their personal stash. Some cops even used the seized alcohol to open their own speaks. The requirement to enforce Prohibition also exhausted the department's resources, leaving too few to fight what the cops thought of as real crimes. As it was for most New Yorkers, for the cops Prohibition was a bad joke. Many of them damned the Anti-Saloon League in their prayers.

Someone in the New York State legislature finally recognized the insanity and four years earlier the policing of Prohibition became the responsibility of federal agents. New York had washed its hands of it at both the state and municipal level.

Duffy had resuscitated himself sufficiently to reminisce about the early days of Prohibition enforcement. As he ordered a second coffee, he asked the waitress to turn up the radio.

"Think I just heard something we need to know, Humph."

"News item: Just moments ago, Mayor Jimmie Walker announced that the transit strike, due to begin today at midnight, had been averted."

"OK, OK," said Humph. "We can get to and from the Bronx on the cheap."

Humph had forgotten about the pending walk-out. In one of the papers he'd seen a photo of what looked like a giant dormitory with hundreds of beds for strike breakers. Now they'd be sent home penniless. Humph had presumed there'd be a strike and it would last until Christmas.

He and Duffy stepped out of the diner. The noon-day July heat had disappeared and the evening looked promising. Humph had been so fixated on Eve that he had done nothing for pleasure in what seemed like weeks. Despite the risk of being led into trouble, Humph still found Duffy amusing. It wasn't as if they'd risk arrest.

Duffy wanted to first go to a speak way up in the Bronx, on 149th Street, just off Third Avenue.

"I did most of my work Downtown or in Harlem. No one would know me in the Bronx." Duffy said.

As the train made its way north, Duffy entertained Humph with stories of Izzy Einstein and Moe Schmidt, two federal agents who became the darlings of the press as they made nearly 5,000 Volstead Act busts.

"If you judged by the papers," Duffy said, "you'd think they were single-handedly draining Manhattan of Evil Booze. They were comical, those two. I saw them at work once at a speak in Brooklyn. I didn't introduce myself as a cop. I just sat back and enjoyed the show. The bartender actually fainted when those funny feds busted him.

"Izzy was so fat he waddled from side to side when he walked. Moe was a lot bigger but he was in no shape to physically threaten anyone. In fact, they were so god-damned ordinary looking and so friendly that at first bartenders never suspected them of being agents. As time went by, some of the bars posted photos of them so they could stay on the alert, but no one could believe that the guys they were face to face with were the famous agents."

Humph said he hadn't heard about them in ages.

"Believe it or not, the feds in Washington got jealous of how much press they were getting nationally compared to the anti-hooch big shots in the nation's capital. They laid them off in some sort of departmental reorganization. I think the pair of them ended up selling insurance or some such thing. Bureaucracy is grand, ain't it?"

After a moment, Duffy added:

"They looked comical. Like clowns. That's how I always saw Prohibition. A farce. Charlie Chaplin should have made a movie about it."

Once again, Humph was finding Duffy more intelligent than most people would think he was. It was not something he wanted to broadcast for some reason. Did that make him a more effective investigator? Perhaps, thought Humph. People would be less worried about what they said around him than they might be when faced with a piercing intelligence eager to trip them up.

Once off the train, they faced a good walk. Humph was hot and perhaps almost as thirsty as Duffy was in any weather. Fortunately, he thought, Duffy seemed to know exactly where he was going. An Irish bloodhound.

The bar was small and gloomy but the patrons were animated. Tea doesn't do that to someone. Observation No. 1: everyone was drinking an alcoholic beverage. Observation No. 2: the bartender gave he and Duffy a sustained stare until they took a seat. Observation No. 3: a middle-aged woman asked if they could afford to buy a poor old lady a cuppa tea. She oozed booze from every pore. She spoke through missing teeth and had an English accent. Duffy obliged her. As he ordered her a drink, he dialed up his true Irish accent. The lady's eyes flashed back-home recognition.

Duffy was a sly one, no doubt about it, thought Humph.

While Humph gratefully gulped his beer, Duffy kept his eye on the woman. After she had half-emptied her glass, he leaned over and in a soft conspiratorial voice said:

"Dearie, would you happen to know if a gent could enjoy the presence of a lady here?"

She returned a lopsided grin.

"You wouldn't be thinking of me, would you, young man?"

"You're a sight to be sure," replied Duffy, "but I have my heart set on a somewhat younger belle. Nothing personal, mind you."

"My cuppa's getting a bit light in the hand…"

Instantly, Duffy scanned the room for the waiter, then yelled, "Hey, lad, over here if it pleases you."

The waiter was in no hurry. He seemed to be enjoying a joke at another table. However, without responding to Duffy directly, he went ahead and filled his order for the lady. Humph wondered whether the waiter was extremely familiar with how she worked. It clearly wasn't her first time in the bar.

A new cuppa in hand, she looked into Duffy's eyes and said:

"For a fine specimen such as yourself, I might very well be able to extend some assistance."

Duffy raised his glass to her and gave her a knowing wink before downing his cup of whiskey.

When the lady finished her drink, she stood as best she could and took Duffy's arm as if he were her escort at a ball. She took him to the far end of the bar where she signaled the barkeep with a raised index finger. Apparently she asked for a door to be opened because she and Duffy promptly disappeared.

When Duffy finally resurfaced, he had his arm around a comely young woman who made a point of granting him devoted looks. They sat at the table. Humph's eyes begged

Duffy for an explanation. Humph wondered whether he was supposed to leave them in peace or stay and observe.

The answer was not long in coming. Duffy suddenly took liberties with the young lady's bosom. She didn't object. As he explored the pleasures, she closed her eyes. Duffy's eyes, however, bore into Humph. No words necessary. See you tomorrow.

As he rose, Humph wasn't at all sure whether Duffy was investigating the availability of girls in such places or simply dispatching his residue hangover with some carnal pleasure.

When Humph got back home, he turned on the radio. He and Duffy had lucked out. The union was now saying that the only thing that had been agreed upon was the reinstatement of 13 of the workers who had been discharged for demonstrating sympathy with the Amalgamated Association of Street and Electric Railway Employees. However, the city had not agreed, they said, to formally recognize that union. Therefore, the strike was still on."

Humph's first thought was whether Duffy was now stuck in the Bronx with no cheap way home. Then he remembered how his former colleague was adept at wrangling himself into and out of any situation. If Duffy took a cab home, he wouldn't be paying for it.

Humph pondered paying a visit the following day to his young friend at the *New York World*. Maybe he could help Humph wind his way through the labyrinth of speakeasies in search of Eve.

He got the idea after reading an article about a group of reporters who had set out two nights before to explore the same world. Their account of the evening made it clear that you could never know what to expect in that world. In one small speak they encountered a gentleman of some cultivation. He was professorial in appearance, the story said. They asked him what he did for a living. He didn't answer but when the newsmen responded to the gentleman's own question—"What are you doing?—

the man said he was most interested in their assignment.

The reporters asked if he would like to take them on a tour of cabarets. He accepted happily. By 7 in the morning, they found themselves at Reubens restaurant and deli on Madison Avenue for some breakfast. The scholarly man told the reporters they should accompany him to Cuba. He admitted that he was in the smuggling business.

"Booze?" assumed one of the reporters. "No, sir. Chinese." The newsmen were obliged to decline the people-smuggling offer. They returned to the newspaper and wrote that no one could say speakeasies weren't interesting.

After reading the account, Humph accepted that he greatly enjoyed it. Becoming a private eye seemed like a great leap forward from pounding a beat. Surely reporting would be interesting, diverse work. He'd get to know the city beyond his little Lower East Side precinct.

However, so far, until this case, being a PI was just as humdrum. As personally painful as this investigation was, he loved its complexity, and even more so loved observing the involvement of decent rich people and despicable rich people hiding inside elegant homes, polishing the image of what America had to offer to the very immigrants the country now despised. They kept on polishing that image but never gave new Americans a hand up.

Humph prided himself in keeping informed of issues. But that wasn't easy. Hot air ruled. Humph had decided that long ago. At least as a cop, he didn't have to cow-tow, although he was well aware of the individuals who could make sure a charge never stuck or a case never got to court.

So far, he had the help of the Women's Bureau. Why not add the Fourth Estate?

As his mind wandered, he latched onto a possibility that had never occurred to him. "I investigate for a living," he told himself. "Reporters, at least the good ones, investigate. Could I become one?" Suddenly annoyed with himself for fantasizing, he threw his legs off the table. Cold, boring pragmatism was a man's only crutch in life.

Humph got up and put on a pot of coffee. He needed to sharpen his mind, not let it paddle around in an ocean of unknowns, drifting with currents he had no control over. As he waited for the coffee, he plunked himself down on a wooden chair that would sustain most people, but not him. He had broken it before.

As he admonished himself for having gotten close to being emotional, a crystal clear image flashed inside his head. It was a totally foreign image of a woman's face. It was pleasant yet unsmiling. He sure as hell didn't know her. Why was she sitting in his brain?

Suddenly, the light went on. The image was sending a message.

"You want a woman in your life. She will never be Sunny, but you need her anyway. Open the door, Humph. Step out of prison."

Humph took the coffee off the stove and went in search of the bottle he always put in an out-of-the-way place.

The thought was unthinkable, he told himself. He had told himself that a thousand times since Sunny left his world. For a second, a minute maybe, he wondered. Could he let himself think otherwise? Did letting another woman into his life mean abandoning Sunny?

"Yes!" he said out loud. The word was like an outburst. It was anger at himself.

When he felt a bourbon calm take hold, Humph realized for the first time that he was the one who still had a life to live, not beautiful Sunny. She would not have wanted him to be a slave to her image.

As true and final as that realization was, Humph felt a ton of sadness descend on him. It squeezed his lungs like a cruel handshake. As the assault dissipated, he poured another drink. He took it to bed.

116

CHAPTER 13

THE next day, Humph walked to the offices of *The World* on Park Row. He had phoned ahead of time and when he arrived the doorman allowed him to pass with just a nod. People tended to remember his hulking figure.

Gerald Franklin, his reporter friend, welcomed him with a grand bow and led him to his desk.

"Tell me, Humph. You have a story for me? I'm going to be cast on the street if I don't come up with something soon."

"I might," said Humph. "I just might. Up to you to decide."

Humph handed him the clipping from his competitor's paper, the column ostensibly about the doings on Broadway that sidestepped into an encounter in a speakeasy with a well-bred man who had a keen interest in a newspaper investigation of speakeasies.

Gerald had read it.

"My first thought upon reading it was finding a way of talking my boss into sending me to Cuba to unearth his people-smuggling operation. I drew a blank. I don't know who this guy is and the story's details were intentionally sketchy in order to protect his identity."

Gerald's face brightened and he moved his chair directly in front of Humph's.

"My dear friend, that paper won't talk to me but…"

"But?" Humph said when the silence became pregnant with surprise.

"But perhaps," said the reporter, "they'd talk to you, an independent investigator nosing about in the world of speaks, just what their paper was doing."

Humph smiled. As the seconds ticked by, the smile got bigger. He had a brainwave. Become a reporter himself.

"Get a press card made for me," he told Gerald.

"What are you talking about, Humph?"

"You heard me. As I investigate this case I'll be acting as a *World* reporter on the sly."

"I'll have to check if we can…"

"Do it," answered Humph.

"The police chief himself has to sign press cards." Gerald's face was pleading.

"Tell him I was one of his finest officers, one who is now fighting crime on a different front."

The press credentials arrived a week later. He had gotten back on good terms with the phone company and was able to get the call from Gerald.

"Just pop in and I'll hand over the press pass." On that same day the press credentials were to be ready, the chief of the Women's Division sent a flatfoot to Humph's place with orders to bring him to her office. The constable arrived in an automobile. Humph didn't spend a second thinking about the royal treatment. He squeezed in beside the driver and said they had to make a quick stop. "Park Row, the

New York World building." The driver, not knowing who Humph was, had no choice but oblige.

Humph pushed his way into the busy newsroom until he found his reporter friend.

Without a hello, Humph stuck out his hand.

"Hurry, I've got a police escort waiting."

It took a moment for the reporter to realize what Humph was talking about.

"Do you mean this?" He held an envelope emblazoned with, "From the Chief of Police, City of New York, NY, U.S.A."

With a friendlier tone and an awkward smile, Humph said:

"Of course, that's what I want. Gotta go."

Back in the police car, Humph stole a peek.

He was now certified as an accredited journalist. It was just a card but for Humph it spoke of a new future. Maybe he'd even a move uptown someday.

The Chief of the Women's Division welcomed Humph to her office. Without exchanging niceties, she announced,

"We've possibly had a modicum of progress."

"Modicum. A good word," thought Humph. He made a mental note to use it as soon as possible to make the word his.

The captain looked as if she were expecting him to ask what the progress was but he remained silent.

When interrogating people, Humph made it a rule to never finish their sentences, nor reach possible conclusions. They would either incriminate themselves or liberate themselves if he allowed them to continue without interruption. That's why, he would argue with Duffy when they were both on the force, it was better to interrogate while sober.

"Patience will never betray you," he'd tell Duffy, adding that, "A drinking man is never patient."

Pissed off, Duffy once called him "preacher man".

Later he said that Humph was probably right.

The captain was forced to reveal what she'd learned.

"One of my girls got her boyfriend to go into a downtown club, on 47^h. She told me her guy hoped to be an actor someday but he worried that his Hell's Kitchen boyhood may have unduly reduced his 'inclination to eloquence'. Those were her words."

Humph suspected that despite her grim countenance, the captain liked telling a yarn.

She went on to say that the young man put on a suit and went to said speakeasy.

"His technique," the captain said, "is to be commended. He ordered several drinks over an hour, ingratiating himself to the serving girls, the hostesses. When one of them thought he was sufficiently primed to invest further in their wares, she offered what she called the extras that good clients deserve. At that moment he suddenly showed himself to be a man of decision. 'I know what I want,' he announced, suddenly standing upright at his table as if preaching a sermon. 'I want your finest girl and her name is Eve!'"

On hearing that, Humph winced.

The captain smiled.

"Overly theatrical, perhaps, but valid under the guise of drunken desire. One of my officers told me when we planned this little operation that the actor's leg had proven hollow in the past. And the club didn't really care. It was noisy anyway and at the prices they charge for drinks, there were undoubtedly few if any limits on customers."

Humph asked the captain about the prices. If he conducted his own survey of speaks, he'd have to know how weighty his billfold would have to be to get him through an evening.

The captain said she didn't know how a much drink cost at the bar in question but knew that police had been called to a speak on Riverside Drive recently.

"Three stockbrokers, wealthy ones at that, were about to tear the place apart after being charged $119 for one round of drinks and sandwiches. From what I was led to understand, the officers calmed things down in short order but declined to ticket the brokers for causing such a ruckus. Their personal addresses, said one of the officers, were more than respectable, by which I think they meant a location that included Park or Fifth Avenue."

Humph said they'd already been penalized enough by the bar bill.

"I'm sure the check was inflated to take into account the fancy attire worn by the three gentlemen," said the captain.

"Anyway, back to our actor. The girls waiting on him hustled about, asking questions of the barkeep, and other important-looking men. They may have been owners. I don't really know. When the girls reassembled around our man, one of them sat on his lap, stroked his whiskers and regretfully informed him that Eve was not on the premises. It turned out that she used to work there as a special dancer, they said, but hadn't been around in about two weeks."

Humph took note of the address of the speak. He asked the captain if Owney Madden owned the joint. The captain didn't know.

"What's next?" Humph asked.

"We go take our actor to more places. At the worst, we'll narrow down the field for you."

"Much appreciated, Captain."

Before going back to the *New York World* and offering his services as a reporter, specialized in speakeasies, gangsters and assorted captains of industry, Humph needed to talk to Duffy, provided Duffy was able to talk after his late night carryings-on in the Bronx. He would tell him what the Captain's girls discovered at one speak.

To Humph's surprise, he found Duffy in fine spirits despite being sober.

"I can't say I furthered our investigation, Humph, but I found a lady who wanted to investigate me, so to speak. Turned out she lives on Delancey so we pooled our resources and returned downtown in style."

Humph couldn't resist asking whether Duffy was on vacation, leave or suspension.

"You haven't talked about a shift in ages."

"Ya shoulda been made detective, Humph, I tell ya. Truth is, I accidentally acquired a respectable allotment of gin for my dear overworked sergeant, who, as you know, is the man who dictates our shifts."

"Say no more, Duff."

After a pause while Duffy did up the laces of his boots and fought off the cigarette smoke that was rising from lips to eyes, Humph asked:

"So, no clues about what happens to girls sucked up by the broker and his mob partner?"

"Yes and no, Humph," replied Duffy, through a deep-down hack the moment he removed the cigarette from his mouth. "I convinced my lady friend through what might have been an excess of Irish charm to inquire as to the whereabouts of an old friend named Eve. The question got an immediate response. 'No!'

"I was about to resign myself to the truth of the matter when in short order two gents in suits stood by my table. One of them, an unsmiling little upstart hiding under his derby, asked if we were there to drink or ask questions. I assured him with a wave of my billy club, which I always carry up my sleeve, that our question about Eve was just that, an old friend's inquiry."

At that point, Duffy said, he and his lady friend decided that drinking was the safest course of action.

Humph needed to think. He paced the room then stood before Duffy.

"Let's go for a walk."

"A walk! In the name of all that's holy, you know damn well that the last thing a sane man ever does is ask a flatfoot to go for a walk on his own time. A beat-walking copper, to go for a walk! That's like asking a professional dancing gal for a personal dance between shows. It just isn't done!"

Humph admitted he had a point. After a few moments of reflection, plus an exploration of his conscience, Humph decided that the search for his Eve justified deviance.

"Duffy, on your feet, old sod. You're coming to an appointment with me where you are going to agree with everything I say. You don't need to be lubricated to do that, do you?"

No response, just a blank stare.

"We're going by taxi if we can find one."

With that, Duffy nodded his head in the affirmative.

"Whatever you say, Humph."

The traffic on the Bowery was so clogged they finally decided to walk to Delancey and a couple of blocks east. There they soon found a taxi. They squeezed themselves into the back seat. The cab was an old Ford. They weren't built for bodies like Humph's.

With his new press credentials, Humph and Duffy breezed past security at the *World*. They were shown to Gerald Franklin's desk.

"I'm getting thirsty," said Duffy.

"You're always thirsty."

It took a full 10 minutes for Humph's friend to arrive. He looked harried.

"Sorry, Humph. Just had three story ideas shot down."

"I hope I can help," offered Humph softly. He didn't want to make promises. He was there with a big ask.

Humph introduced him to Officer Duffy.

"He's one of the city's finest," said Humph. "Worked with him for years."

Gerald nodded and offered his hand.

"Welcome to the *World*."

Getting no response, Franklin added that it was an inside joke at the paper.

Humph quickly explained his offer.

"Now that I am an accredited journalist, I have a proposition for you and your paper. For police reasons, personal reasons and journalistic reasons..." Humph paused to catch his breath. "For those reasons, Gerald, I want to investigate and report on not only speakeasies, which I know are old news at the paper, but the uppity-ups and the mobsters who run them. Worse, and this is the real story, Gerald, these bastards use their speaks as a place to display their working girls."

Humph continued in what for him was as close as he ever got to making a speech.

"Not only that, but Prohibition has also been a boon to gangster-run bordellos. They can't get enough girls to service their new joints. Guys don't have to prowl the streets anymore hoping to find a lady under a streetlamp. They only have to go to their favorite speak for a drink. The girls are all but on the menu at many of them."

Gerald stopped slumping in his chair.

"This is for real?" he asked.

"You know I was a cop. In fact, you know a lot more about me than that."

Humph paused, then looked straight into the eyes of the young newspaperman.

"And I'm sorely tempted to even the scales by finding out more about your personal life." Humph let the shock set in. Then he laughed, his very own little laugh, the corners of his mouth lifting ever so slightly and with a sound that resembled someone clearing their throat.

Humph was high. The scent of the hunt was in his nostrils.

Franklin smiled.

"I can't assign such a big investigation without approval but I love it, Humph."

"Wait. This man here, Officer Duffy, is your cinching argument. He's still on the force and he's a bulldog when it comes to investigating. I haven't the time to tell you about all the biggies he's brought down. I've explained my goals in this case and he's on board. In fact, he's got special… what do you call it?...dispensation from the NYPD to pursue this. If we succeed, Franklin, the NYPD looks good and they damn well know it."

Gerald darted from his chair. Humph could hear him yelling, "Where's the city editor." Men on the City Desk shrugged their shoulders. Franklin then ran into the managing editor's office at the back end of the newsroom. It was too far away for Humph to hear anything.

It was 20 minutes before Franklin returned to his desk. Duffy was fidgeting but fortunately his kept his word and kept his mouth shut. "He's got the screaming meemies," Humph thought. His next thought wasn't for his friend but for his own thankfulness for having deserted the force.

Gerald returned, almost skipping like a boy as he dodged around *World* staffers. He threw his arms wide open and exclaimed, "Sold!"

"The M.E. loved the idea."

Humph returned a blank look.

"M.E. Managing Editor, Humph. He said you've got free rein and on top of that, Humph, you're now on salary. Twenty-seven dollars a week! He figured a guy with your background and contacts is just what the paper needs right now. We're getting beat on stories every second day."

To Humph's ears, $27 was a handsome hunk of change.

"What about me?" Duffy said, testily.

Calmly, Gerald reminded him that he was employed by the NYPD and that he was simply doing his duty, his "much appreciated duty".

Duffy kept his mouth shut but gave a baseball umpire's "out" gesture, arm raised, thumb extended backwards.

"Got to go, Gerald. I owe you big. You won't regret this."

Gerald smiled and cringed simultaneously as Humph shook his hand.

Humph then turned his attention to the still-seated Duffy. He took his hand, raised him to his feet and slapped his arm around Duffy's shoulders. He promptly marched him out of the building. On the street, he said:

"Name your bar."

"Your place," said Duffy.

Humph contemplated his new-found wealth and didn't hesitate. They walked back down to Chinatown and then down to a basement apartment on Henry Street. They emerged with two bottles of bourbon. The real thing. They weren't cheap but Humph was cracking his shell. He had been injected with something, at the paper and at the captain's office. He'd never felt such respect.

His thoughts were bubbling far too rapidly to know what he was truly feeling. He would be embarrassed to admit it but at this very moment he felt he was leading the cavalry. The press. The police. He'd unearth Eve by hook or by crook. The usually verbose Irishman by his side didn't dare speak.

A triple shot of bourbon, eagerly quaffed, broke the silence.

"While the captain's girls and their actor companion make their way to a few more speakeasies," Humph suggested, "I think we should see what dirt we can get on my broker acquaintance, Mr. Reginald Ostenbruch. We want to also verify any business operations he might be sharing with Owney Madden."

Duffy refilled his own glass and Humph's. Before sitting again, he looked down at Humph, slouching under the influence of his massive initial blast of Bourbon.

"A tall order, Humph. You already told me there's little chance the pudgy broker will willingly palaver with the likes of you again. Worn out your welcome, I'd say."

"True enough," said Humph.

"And as for Owney, the only way of tying him to speaks is to tail his trucks. The boys at the precinct know where we should start because they've busted up his warehouses on more than one occasion. But as for putting Madden and Ostenbruch in the same stew, I don't rightly know how to start."

Humph suddenly remembered the obliging secretary from Ostenbruch's office, the one who passed him documents over tea, ones that showed her boss's Gramercy Park address. He let his mind wander and remembered the affectionate little wave she gave him as she returned to work.

"Edith," Humph said. "Edith Fitzsimmons."

"What on earth are you talking about, Humph?"

"Sorry, Duff. Didn't realize I was thinking out loud. Edith Fitzsimmons is Ostenbruch's secretary. She helped me set up my first interview with him when I wanted to find out what his connection was with Eve."

Humph proffered that she had taken a shine to him and therefore would likely be willing to take another risk or two in getting her hands on the broker's other dealings, if indeed he keeps them at his office.

"Worth a try, lover boy," said Duffy.

Then Humph remembered a name that came up when he first started looking into so-called bucket shops.

"I've been neglecting the lad horribly," said Humph, "but what put me on to brokerages and eventually Ostenbruch was a client, the son of a millionaire businessman. He got himself finessed out of 10 grand by a bogus brokerage. He wanted me to unearth the culprit. Long story short, Duff, I made some inquiries into the kid's father. I ended up finding out that he does a lot of so-far-unexplained business in Montreal, the home of some pretty damn good whiskey."

Humph admitted it was idle speculation of his part but he wondered whether by chance the kid's dad imported booze for Madden's joints. He also guessed that Ostenbruch would know of him because people on Wall Street always make a point of knowing the city's richest inhabitants.

"Then when Eve didn't show up after a couple of days I put my client's case aside and decided this was not the time to be looking for a Montreal connection with illegal booze imports and the even slimmer possibility that Ostenbruch, let alone Madden, was involved."

While Humph ran down the stages of his investigation, Duffy got up and walked around the room. He sat for a moment on Humph's bed. Then he lay down. Humph was going to tell him this was not time to sleep but then he saw that Duffy's eyes were wide open, staring at the ceiling. He was thinking.

"You were right," Duffy said, getting to his feet. "Making the bootlegging and brothel bust would put more flowers in our bonnet than we could handle. But that wouldn't necessarily get us an inch closer to your girl Eve."

He asked if Humph had a photograph of her.

"I do," said Humph. "But just one, taken some years back with her mom and me. I don't know whether that will help much. I also have a painting of her."

Duffy said nothing and Humph headed to a closet near his bed. He disappeared inside it. Duffy heard some things falling to the floor and he heard Humph curse. Finally Humph emerged with the photo and a framed canvas.

Sheepishly, he told Duffy he couldn't bear seeing Sunny's image day and night. He handed both to Duffy.

"A looker, Humph. No wonder her girl's so pretty."

Humph surprised Duffy by pouring them both another drink. As Humph handed him the glass, he saw that Humph's face was suddenly betraying the pain of just holding the photo.

Finally, Humph asked:

"What do we do?"

CHAPTER 14

THE next day, Duffy surprised his desk sergeant by showing up at the precinct station.

"Make me an acting detective," he said.

"No can do, Duff. Regs and all that crap."

"I've got a case that needs investigating full time, round the clock."

The sergeant asked Duffy how long it had been since his last drink. Then accepting that his officer was sober, he asked for details, adding, "Just the essentials, mind you. No Irish oratory called for."

"Just hear me out before you answer," Duffy said, all but making it an order.

"A young woman was kidnapped a few weeks back, a pretty girl, a burlesque performer and sometime stripper.

This is where you keep your yap shut, sarge! She's a fine young lady and the step-daughter of one of our own. What complicates everything is that some shady and influential people may very well be behind the kidnapping. It would be a mighty fine feather in our cap if we nailed them. Now you can speak."

"You're a right uppity bogger, aren't ya."

Duff took no offense. The sarge had some green blood as well. Though the city's large Irish population was guilty of unpardonable bias against later immigrants, such as Italians and Jews from Eastern Europe, they in turn received more than their fair share of abuse by the wealthier non-Catholic white population that outright opposed all immigration. Duff and the sarge enjoyed publicly dumping on their own heritage. They thought it showed everyone else they had thick skins and wouldn't run from any confrontation.

"What I need," said Duffy, "is the best information we have on big-shot bad guys." He named Ostenbruch and Madden and Randall Overton, the magnate with likely Montreal connections.

"Meet you at the local this evening, when my shift's done," said the sergeant.

While Duffy was ordering his superior officer around, Humph ambushed his secretary contact just before close of business. She was more than happy to see him. He took her to a diner for supper, soup and peach pie. To his delight, she announced: 'I haven't given up, Humph!'

She explained that she had found a documented link between the broker and Owney. A receipt from a trucking company, made out to the broker. The bill was huge, about $2,000.

'But I didn't stop there,' she told Humph. "Goodness, this pie is delicious. Sorry, look what I found."

She wrapped her hand around a wad of papers in her purse.

"I went down to city hall's record's department. The trucking company is registered to none other than OM Éire Enterprises. At the time it meant nothing to me but I kept looking. OM Éire Enterprises owns 17 companies in New York. It's never clear in the records what the companies do but I wrote down the addresses."

The woman was a godsend, thought Humph. He couldn't have done a better job of investigating.

"Why?" Humph asked. "Has your boss ever treated you badly?"

"No," Edith answered, looking away from Humph. "I did it for you." She looked at him as she said it and immediately dropped her eyes.

Humph bit his tongue. He had been about to ask, "But why do it for me?" It dawned on him that she wasn't just a sweet, good-hearted soul trying to help a criminal investigation because it was the right thing to.

It had been a long time since a woman had made Humph that uncomfortable. He stammered. "Edith, you see…", but he couldn't finish the sentence. He had no idea how to.

Finally, he said: "More pie?"

She squeezed his hand. He admitted that he was partial to peach pie as well. His paralytic shyness didn't bother her in the slightest.

For the next half hour, they talked about the weather, the smell of horse manure that remained on the streets despite the explosion of Ford motor cars. And Edith informed him that on this very day Henry Ford announced a new four-cylinder Model T. They laughed about walking next to a New York City Sanitation truck that still had open compartments for the trash tossed in resentfully by grossly underpaid workers. There were new trucks, which had come into service just this year, ones that allowed the garbage to be hidden from view and smell.

Humph walked her home to a nondescript four-unit tenement on Maiden Lane.

He lightly retrieved her hand from here side and said he didn't know how to thank her for her invaluable investigation. Edith gave a feigned curtsy and shut him up with a big, laughing smile.

"Yes," she said, when Humph was clearly speechless. "You may call on me."

Humph took the key from her hand and opened the door for her. She took his right hand, retrieving the key but using the gesture to give his hand a squeeze. Then she disappeared.

Humph was happily perplexed all the way home.

When he entered his own apartment, the first thing he saw was the photo of Sunny and the painting of Eve, the ones he'd shown Duffy. The confusion of feelings was too much. He grabbed them and returned them to the closet. He sat down at his table and tried to think about the case. At one point, he pounded the table. Later he thought he did that to wake himself up to the present, to stop remembering the past, to stop picturing the future. Whatever the reason, he decided, he had only one course to follow. Eve.

He began looking at the documents he'd just received from Edith. In them he saw connection after connection. Owney, Mr. OM, was going to be his. He began to read the incorporation papers in detail. At precisely 2:49 a.m.—it was so important that Humph wrote it down— he saw the sweetest sentence he'd ever read. Owner: OM Éire Enterprises, Newark, NJ. Nominal owner: Reginald Ostenbruch, CEO, New York, NY. Headquarters: Kingston, Jamaica.

Humph guessed that while the real owner of the enterprise was Madden, registering the company under Ostenbruch as the nominal owner shielded the gangster from prying eyes.

They were married. They were a pair. Linked and liable for distribution and sale of an illegal substance. And, more importantly, the proprietors of speakeasies where women cost not much more than a bottle of Canadian whiskey.

The next day it was Duffy's turn to wake up Humph.

When Humph opened the door, his first words were "Shut up." He then shuffled into his so-called kitchen to put on the kettle and prepare coffee.

It was a full 10 minutes by Duffy's reckoning before the big man said:

"Me first."

Humph took Duffy by the shoulders and forcefully led him to a chair.

"Quiet, Duff, for God's sake. I have news!"

"Shove it, Humph, for God's sake. So do I!"

"I'm a helluva lot bigger than you so I go first!"

Duffy had never seen Humph that emotional or absurd.

Humph started at the beginning of the evidence that not only linked Madden and Ostenbruch but also pointed to a large-scale, diverse trucking operation that more than likely transported booze.

"A bust like that would get us all the leverage we need to unearth Eve." Instantly, Humph regretted his choice of words. He added, as if it were part of the same sentence, "need to find out where they've got her working."

Humph then tossed Edith's pile of documents on Duffy's lap.

"Proof," Humph said, "that Owney and the broker are joined at the hip."

Duffy wasn't much of a reader but he dove into the evidence he'd just been handed. Humph's eyes were growing heavy by the time Duffy finally spoke.

"Humph, you and your new love deserve the credit for this stuff."

"Edith is not my…"

"A slip of the tongue, Humph. I was just speculating inside my head, if you know what I mean, and picturing myself throwing all this down in front of my sergeant. He would see in an instant that I'd hit goal with my investigation. He'd then show it all to the lieutenant. At that moment, I'd call the sarge aside and remind him to recommend me for the detective's exam. Who knows, Humph, maybe they'd be so impressed by my work they'd say, 'Fuck the exam.'"

Humph couldn't resist laughing.

"If you dream like that sober, Duff, heaven knows what you dream of drunk."

"Would you mind, Humph, if I sort of took the credit?"

"Not at all, Duff. I'm not on the force and finding Eve is all I care about. Pat yourself on the back for a brilliant investigation."

"I owe ya, Humph. And an Irishman never forgets a debt. You know that."

"That I do, Detective Duffy."

Duffy shot to his feet after placing all the documents in a neat pile.

"I'd dearly love to stake you to a drink or two right now, Humph, but I'd better get this stuff into safer hands at the precinct station,"

Humph now had to wait for the captain's matrons to infiltrate more speakeasies in search of Eve. In the meantime, he wanted to see young Frankie and assure him he was still on the case. Maybe, the kid would be able to shed more light on his father's businesses, especially in Montreal. After that, back to Park Avenue for the same purpose.

CHAPTER 15

HUMPH awoke to an angry rain. Someday he'd have money for cabs. He didn't usually indulge in wishful thinking but slumping over the morning's first coffee facilitated the flight of fancy. During it, his inner eye fell momentarily on Edith as well. A piercing curse from the street woke him from the imaginings. He looked out the window and saw a man in a street vendor's apron chasing a kid. He didn't stand a chance of catching the little thief. The vendor gave up and yanked off his apron. He pulled it over his bald head to protect it from the rain.

Humph's first stop was the captain's office. He wanted to inform her of the evidence that had been placed in Duffy's hands linking the gangster and the broker.

"Just a heads-up, Cap."

She said her girls had been busy, although for a while they'd have to work on their own because the young actor who'd been helping them got savagely punched out at one establishment.

"But worry not, Humph. My girls are resourceful and determined. Anything beats being at home wielding a heavy flat iron while you breastfeed your little one."

Humph gathered she was on the road to spinsterhood by intent.

Before leaving, he used her phone to call Frankie. The kid wanted to meet at a gentleman's club in Midtown.

"Why?" asked Humph.

"For my father, I would venture, being in places like the venerable Union Club, was akin to heaven on earth. As a boy, I recall him often announcing he had affairs to attend to at the club. Might jog memories for me."

Because of the weather, Humph was glad to be able to stay downtown. The club was located on 37ᵗʰ Street at Fifth Avenue, a convenient bus ride south of his next appointment, on Park Avenue.

Arrogantly large Victorian-era buildings all looked gloomy to Humph's eye. They may be staffed to the gills but they aways appeared empty and drafty. The ghosts of self-important, self-righteous people did a poor job indeed of hinting that there was once true life between those predictably decorated walls and under those absurdly high ceilings that made a room impossible to heat.

Upon arriving in the lounge, a servant of some sort announced the arrival of Mr. Humphrey Barstal. In response to an almost invisible hand gesture from Frankie, a good 30 feet away, the servant directed him to the member's table.

Frankie stood. Immediately, Humph knew the smile on his face was genuine. It wasn't one of happiness but simply one that bespoke a sincere welcome, a far cry from the besotted condescension of their very first meeting in Frankie's old apartment.

"Shall we get right down to business?" Frankie sounded eager. To Humph's regret, he had little news to impart to the boy. He had news, tons of it with regard to his overall investigation, but nothing that nailed a broker to the wall. Humph decided then and there, on instinct, to level with Frankie. The kid was being straight with him. He owed him the same in return.

"At the outset, Frankie, our goal was to find out who bamboozled you. It then became a question of why and who was behind it because it made no sense that a well-known broker would participate in what was essentially a scam, and now a very illegal one. A law was passed in the early 20s outlawing bucket shops."

Frankie said nothing.

Humph continued.

"This is hard for me to say, Frankie, because I take my investigator's job very seriously. My duty is to my client. Always. But this time, Frankie, my heart got waylaid. My investigation into the broker Ostenbruch led me directly to a personal tragedy that I don't know how to deal with, let alone solve."

Still Frankie said nothing.

"I learned that my daughter…well, she's my stepdaughter, though not officially…"

"Doesn't matter, Humph. Go on."

She had been previously acquainted with Ostenbruch. She was a dancer and he had started hanging out at her shows and tipping her big. That's not unusual, Frankie, but my Eve, that's her name, Eve, she said he started insisting. Twice he broke into her dressing room. Because he looked like a gentleman, and clearly had means, she hesitated on calling the big boys who the theater hires for just such invasions. Finally, she told me, he showed up at her place. How he got the address, she has no idea. Next thing I know, Frankie, is that she's gone. That was weeks ago. Eve and I are like that," he said, crossing his fingers.

Humph then leaned back into the easy chair. He'd been sitting on the edge while detailing the case.

"It's all related somehow, you, your money, your dad and the bastard broker, and my Eve. But I don't know how. Not yet, anyway. The cops are also working on it."

Frankie never took his eyes off Humph. Finally he said,

"It's all OK, Humph. Your girl is more important than my 10 grand. They don't even compare."

Humph could barely believe the boy's sudden maturity, from a spoiled, selfish brat blessed with so much money it meant nothing, to a human being capable of empathy.

"You're not the man I met in the flat in the Bronx." Humph's statement of fact elicited a tiny smile of gratitude.

"I've turned my back on Dear Papa. Yes, I still have his money but the only thing I care about now is becoming a writer. I told you that at the Plaza bar. What's different now is that I'm writing for a living. Well, not that I need the money, but I have a real job as a writer. I work for CBS. I am in the writing pool. We churn out radio plays like there's no tomorrow. I'm just learning but guess what, Humph, I'm getting paid to write."

Humph's stare could not shatter the pride that Frankie's eyes reflected.

"Can I make a confession, Frankie?"

Frankie nodded eagerly.

"I have always dreamed of being a writer. Really. God's truth. But I never dared try. You, though, Frankie, you did it, you did it for real. Bravo, son."

"Maybe someday I'll write a radio play about this case. From what you've told me so far, Humph, about all the complications and connections, we could make a serial out of it."

Humph looked down at his hands.

Frankie quickly sensed the offence he'd caused, again something that would not have happened short months ago.

"I didn't mean to make light of the case, Humph. It's just that I'm really excited about this incredible career I've embarked on. I feel alive when I'm making up things and other people get it. Believe me, Humph, the reality I had before, the one you got a glimpse of, that was as bloodless as a hangman's heart."

Humph said nothing but inside he hoped someday that he could write a line like that.

"Anyway, Frankie, I wanted to let you know I haven't forgotten you. Mostly I wanted to tell you that your case is part of a much bigger one. I just hope it doesn't turn out to be a deadlier one."

Frankie nodded his understanding.

"You're going to have to just wait. As I said, the cops are going to speakeasies one by one trying to uncover the ones that offer girls to guys as chasers for their whiskey. A bunch of women cops have gone undercover in the bars."

"Didn't know there was such a thing as women cops," said Freddie.

"Yeah, apparently they've been around for a while. Might make a radio script for you Frankie," Humph said with his trademark quarter smile.

"And how!"

Humph got serious again and reminded him that all this was part of a larger investigation into bootlegging and prostitution. We got information that might connect a gangster to your friend and mine, the broker who bilked you out of $10,000. However, we still have to prove it."

Frankie said he was impressed.

Humph could tell he was now all ears.

"All of which leads me to a delicate matter, Frankie. As I went over documents that might connect the gangster and the broker, what caught my attention is that your dad is always going to Montreal, where New York speaks get the whiskey they can sell at premium rates. Your dad knows our bastard broker friend. Does he also know

Owney Madden, the gangster I mentioned a moment ago? The cops already have proof that Madden and Ostenbruch have trucking operations in common. Do their fleets pull up to loading docks in Montreal? Or is it remotely possible that your dad ships them what they want from a distillery he owns most of in Montreal?"

Frankie fielded the hardball question as elegantly as the Yankees' Lou Gehrig.

"What an intriguing thought," said Frankie. "Stuffed-shirt Papa, a man whose religion is appearances with a capital A, waltzing at the Ritz with gangsters and smugglers. I've been to Montreal, not just as a kid with Dad but as an adult. It's quite the town."

Humph had never been north of the border. Maybe there would be something there to investigate after all. Suddenly he sat bolt upright and cleared his throat loudly. He'd been blindsided by a thought, a thought he didn't create. The words that sent him wheezing were: "Edith would probably like that."

"You OK, Humph?"

"Yes. Must have forgotten to breathe for a moment."

Frankie said he didn't know anything about his father's operations in Montreal but he might be able to get some information out of one of his dad's lawyers, the one who oversaw his withdrawals from the trust his father had set up for him. Having the trust, which Frankie could withdraw from, greatly reduced the unpleasantness of being pestered by the boy for money.

"I'll tell him the lawyer that business matters were starting to appear more attractive. 'Knowledge of Papa's holdings would guide me along the right path.' Our lawyer would have to agree."

Humph said every little bit of information might be useful.

"So be it," said Frankie. "Let's adjourn for the day. I have some script ideas to work on."

They shook hands on the steps outside the club. Frankie asked the doorman to hail him a taxi. Humph walked down to the street and continued over to Fifth Avenue. He rooted a nickel out of his pocket and stepped aboard the next bus, a green and yellow affair owned by the Fifth Avenue Coach Company. It was famous for having reduced its fare from 10 cents to five cents just a few years earlier.

The sun was now shining but it wasn't hot so Humph climbed up to the open roof seats. As always, traffic was infernally congested on the avenue. Humph didn't care. The interview with Franklin had been pleasant and promising.

A few blocks north, he saw a traffic tower for the first time. Fifth Avenue was not part of his regular itinerary. As a former cop, he wondered what he would have thought of being perched 23 feet above the street on one of the seven brass towers erected on the avenue a few years back in an attempt to keep traffic moving. The newspapers originally described them as marvelous inventions, and perhaps they were, but already dissent was tarnishing the glory of the innovation. Each of the ornate towers not only directed traffic flow. They also had telephones, push-button signals, and flashlights for the policeman operating the tower. The icing on the cake, said the papers, were illuminated clocks equipped with bells, which sounded every hour. Humph had never lived anywhere but New York but he couldn't believe any other city in the world could have come up with this development. The problem was that traffic didn't flow any faster.

His trip to see Colin took forever. New York traffic was impossible and would always be.

As the bus sat idle for minutes at a time, numerous passengers decided to get off and walk to their destinations. Humph picked up a newspaper left behind by one of them. Bootlegging was in the news again.

The so-called Prince of Bootleggers, William V. Dwyer, the already convicted leader of a $25 million rum ring, got a police escort to a train bound for Atlanta where he would serve his sentence. Some of the local bootleggers tied to his operation were also sentenced to jail for failure to pay taxes on bootleg profits.

The story, thought Humph, looked good as a headline but meant nothing in the end. And every cop knew it. The convictions amounted to grains of sand in a huge universe of New York speakeasies, beloved by high society and the immigrant poor.

By the time the bus reached 67th Street, Humph was glad to get off. The swaying and the stopping, starting and sudden braking, and the grating declarations of impatience by New York drivers wanting to get by the bus, left him weary though all he'd done was sit.

The doorman at Colin's building now recognized the towering investigator.

"Good afternoon, sir." Sunshine glinted from his epaulettes as he opened the door for Humph. Humph didn't like people opening doors for him but he nodded his thanks to the doorman anyway. Doormen were among a detective's best friends, right up there with bartenders. The former monitored the rich, the latter specialized in the doings of thugs and bimbos. Humph always made sure he had a good supply of aces in his pocket to resurrect memories.

Colin didn't appear at the door to greet him this time. Not that Humph minded because it was Rebecca who ushered him inside. Humph was about to say, "Thank you, Rebecca," only to remember that Colin said she didn't recognize her name if he didn't roll the R. Humph wasn't about to embarrass himself by trying.

When Colin appeared, he was sweating and holding a large medicine ball.

"I have my own gym, right here in my own apartment. This is the first time I've used it. I was hoping Rebecca would join me but she insisted she had work to do." Colin laughed.

"Progress?" he asked Humph, wiping his forehead with an oversized white towel.

"Yes and no. Everyone's working hard but so far no Eve. However, we're starting to make a few paper connections between Madden and Ostenbruch. As for your spiritual leader in the world of high finance, Mr. Randall Overton, we have proof that he owns a distillery in Montreal.

"The next step would be proof of sales to Madden or at least deliveries involving the two. To that end, I talked to his son again and he just might come up with what we need.

"He said he'd forgotten to mention in our previous meetings that he gets money every month from a trust his father set up because his father got tired of his do-nothing son bugging him all the time for money. Now they have no reason to meet face to face, which I gather suits both of them.

"Anyway, there is an intermediary, a family lawyer. He's the one who effectively runs the trust and showers the kid with money. Frankie, the old man's son, said he knows the lawyer well. He's been their family lawyer forever and Frankie thinks he might be able to get some information from him about his father and Madden. Frankie's plan is to tell the lawyer that he's reconsidering his refusal to go into business now that he was getting more mature and all that. He would emphasize the fact that he knew he had much to learn. Could the lawyer help him by showing him how his father has set up his businesses? Frankie figures the lawyer will be more than willing because he knows the old man always wanted a son to someday take over his business."

"Sounds good," said Colin.

"Very good," Humph agreed. "However, once again I can only wait until I hear from him. What he learns might dovetail nicely with the stuff you gave me. The cops are already looking into that."

Humph asked Colin if by chance he knew the family lawyer and whether he appeared to be the type who would open up to his boss's son.

"Never set eyes on him to my knowledge, Humph. Sorry. Speaking of sorry, Humph, Rebecca and I were about to spend the afternoon playing Sorry. Care to join us?"

The offer drew a complete blank from Humph.

"Whatever that is, sorry but no."

"It's a board game, Humph. It's called Sorry. Wildly popular."

"Sorry again, but all I heard was the word 'bored.'"

As Humph made his way back home, he was elated to have so many irons in the fire. Surely, one of them at least would pay off big. Then he realized that his optimism didn't apply to Eve's disappearance.

The following day was interminable. Lots of irons in the fire but he wasn't stoking any of them at the moment. The Women's Bureau was on the hunt for Eve. Duffy and his boys at the precinct station were busy exploring the paper trail between the broker and the gangster. Frankie was presumably picking the lawyer's brain to find a way to put a noose around his own father's neck.

Suddenly Humph remembered that he was now a reporter. His spirits soared. He dug his billfold out of his jacket. He removed the $11 worth of aces he carried to bribe informants. Finally, his fingers felt the press card. He removed it gently and placed it on the kitchen table.

Glancing down at the card from time to time, Humph slouched on his wooden chair and wondered how he could write about the investigation. He couldn't say the police were investigating Ostenbruch or Madden, even though they were always supposedly investigating Madden for a flotilla of felonies committed over the years. He certainly couldn't name Frankie's dad. Both he and the paper would be sued faster than a lawyer could bring a smile to his lips. Yes, he could write that a burlesque performer was missing and presumed kidnapped. He'd already decided that he would refer to Eve as a burlesque performer and not a stripper when it came time to publish a story. But doing so would endanger the undercover policewomen crawling through speakeasies asking about a gal named Eve.

No, it wasn't time to dig out a pen and ink. For a moment he pictured himself pounding away at a typewriter keyboard like the boys at the *World*. That quickly gave way to a snorted laugh as he realized typing with his big fingers would be like playing a piano with a boot on each hand. Maybe when the time came to write his first story he could dictate the facts to a reporter, then look over his shoulder to make sure he got it right, especially the parts about his girl. He'd ask his contact about it on his next visit to Park Row.

Humph liked to keep moving. On his own, he was restless. He had an ordered mind but a wind-up toy of a body. It wouldn't let him lie about the apartment, let alone nap.

He turned on the radio. The sound of a Brahms étude filled his room. Classical and opera were more popular than ever, he'd read in a radio magazine. He bought a copy after Frankie said he was entering the world of airwaves. Only dance music drew more listeners. Humph liked both. He liked radio now that he didn't have to wear a headset or fiddle with the dial or lean forward to try to make out the words that magically came across the space. He grew up hearing classical music and there was plenty of it on radio. After getting a modern radio, he thought record companies were stupid charging premium prices for classical recordings. On radio you could listen to a long work without having to get up mid-performance and put on another record. The thing he hated most about the new medium was the abundance of religious shows. He'd grown up with Jewish parents who made a point of not imposing their religion on anyone. The only time he'd ever been in a church was in the course of investigating a stolen collection box at a church on Hester Street.

Humph didn't get a chance to hear the end of the concert. A loud banging at his door got him to his feet. A friend wouldn't knock that way. He picked up his billy club. He yanked the door open prepared to threaten whoever was on the other side.

It was a cop.

"Why on God's earth were you hammering at the door? I'm not deaf."

The constable looked no more than 18. He stammered that he had an important message from the chief of the Women's Bureau.

"Well, what's the message?" Humph demanded.

"I wrote it down," said the cop, handing a slip of paper to the giant before him.

It read:

"We know where Eve is. Meet me first thing in the a.m."

CHAPTER 16

THERE were two chairs in front of the captain's desk. When Humph arrived, a woman was sitting in one of them. The captain pointed to the other chair.

"Humph, meet Karena." Then, looking at Karena, she said, "Say hello to Humph, just Humph. He gets angry if you call him by his birth name…"

Humph held up his hand before she could tell Karena his name was Humphrey.

Karena nodded to Humph, then stood and extended her hand. Humph had never seen a woman do that. For a second Humph hesitated, then took her hand in his paw.

"Karena Melchinskaya. Ukrainian if you're wondering."

"Karena and the actor lush have already hit 11 speaks," said the captain. "My other officers have hit 47 in total.

Then last night our actor friend made his usual drunken 'I want Eve!' speech. I'll let Karena tell you about her night."

Karena turned her chair to better face Humph while she repeated the statement she'd given the captain:

She said a serving girl told him to sit down. As she did so her hand brushed his cheek and he obliged immediately.

"'Eve, you say?'"

"I told her yes before the actor could mumble a word.

"She said she knew an Eve but she didn't know if she was the girl we wanted.

"Again, I made sure to be the one to answer.

"I described the girl as pert as all get out. Even pretty. Outspoken. A sweetheart in the end. Brunette. Hair straight. No bob for her. Too independent to follow fashion.

"The young waitress laughed.

"She said, 'Pardon my bob, miss, but there's nothing wrong with fashion if it liberates a lady.'

"I said Eve's one of a kind.

"I held the girl's gaze for a moment, then asked whether we were now talking about the same girl.

"The waitress actually grinned. That made me think that if we were talking about the same person, the two of them are friends.

"She answered, 'I think so.'

"Then ignoring my order to keep silent, the actor asked if he could see her.

"The waitress looked at him. Her eyes were suddenly suspicious.

"I was furious at him.

"I said it was me who wanted to say Hi.

"The server replied that she was with somebody right then. She said she couldn't interrupt but she'd keep an eye out. She said she was with one of the bosses.

"Half an hour later, the server returned with two more drinks, ordered with a hand signal by the actor.

"She said she was sorry but there was still no sight of her or the boss. She said she was going on break.

"I wasn't going to sit another half hour with the half-stewed actor. I opened my bag and surreptitiously checked the photo of Eve. I then got up and casually made my way to the hallway the server had used.

"There were several doors but I could hear no sound coming from them. At the end of the hall were stairs behind a door. I only saw the stairs when a man exited the door and passed by me, leering all the while. The place was disgusting.

"The stairs were narrow. I wondered whether I'd get to the top and find myself in the middle of an orgy. But an orgy, I realized, would produce a lot more noise than what I was hearing. Just a few voices, male and female. The floor creaked loudly in places but I continued, almost tiptoeing.

"At the back of the hallway, at the last door on the right, a woman's voice said, 'Get your fucking hands off me.' She was angry. Her words came out almost like a growl.

"The man replied, 'That anyway to treat your benefactor, baby?'

"My heart was beating so hard it hurt. I just had to get a look at the woman inside. I decided not to knock and simply let myself into the room. In an instant the man jumped from the side of the bed and stood before me. 'Who do you think you are, whore?'

"I said I was very sorry. I said I thought I heard a friend's voice. I owe her money. I didn't know she had company. I said a server told me my friend was here, at the club.

"I held my breathe for the two or three seconds it took to find out whether my unthought-out words would get me a fist in the face or a chance to have a word with the girl.

"The man turned for a second to look at the woman sitting on the bed. My eyes followed his. I thought, 'It could be. It could be.' Then the man all but screamed at me. 'Get out, whore! You don't get to come in here unless I call for you. Go!'

"I backed out of the room, realizing the bastard thought I worked there as one of his ladies for hire.

"I quickly made my way down the stairs and through the hallway that led to the bar. I raised my arm to signal the actor but his eyes were locked on a hostess two tables away. When I got to the table I smacked the actor on the back of the neck. I suppose I shouldn't have done that but my nerves were shot and I was still angry with him.

"We're going…now!" I told him.

"I all but pushed him across the street to an all-night diner. We took a table by the window. The idiot actor said he wasn't hungry.

"I told him we weren't there to eat for Christ's sake.

"I ordered coffee for him and a juice for myself. It was the first of many because we sat there half the night. The actor fell asleep with his head on the table.

"I remember thinking it would be a job and a half getting him home, or at least back to the precinct station and a bed in a cell.

"When traffic in and out of the club petered out entirely, I could only conclude that the girl called Eve either lived there or was staying the night with the owner, if that's what he really was. I say that because the server had said 'one of our owners.'"

Humph stood. Although his emotions were set to explode, he knew he had to let Karena's detailed account of the encounter sink in. The officer's discovery was everything he'd dreamed of, namely that Eve was alive. That's all that mattered, at least for now. But Eve had to be rescued. His mind went blank.

He turned back to face the captain.

"Promote this officer." It sounded like an order. When he realized that, he continued in a normal voice:

"And give her a medal for bravery."

"I'm already considering it, Humph," said the captain, sensing the load that had just been lifted from his shoulders.

CHAPTER 17

AFTER leaving the police station, Humph went looking for Charles Duffy. If Duff has had even half the success of Karena, thought Humph, he'd tell them to make him a detective, too, and without bothering with any kind of exam. At the precinct station, he learned that Officer Duffy had just left, supposedly on his way home. The officer Humph spoke with said Duffy had been piling up the hours on some case or other.

"Some case or other" could only mean their case, Eve, the bootleggers and the brokers. But since Duff hadn't tried to reach him it was unlikely he'd made much progress. Humph decided to let him get some sleep. Humph started home himself but after a few steps decided to run one check to see if Duff had gone home. He looked in at the local cop bar. He was so excited about the news he'd just received that a drink would go down well. Lindbergh may have just crossed the Atlantic in a plane but Humph wasn't comfortable with his feet off the ground. It was time to land.

A quick glance down the bar of the narrow establishment told him Duff wasn't officiating. Humph ordered a double bourbon, which he consumed standing at the bar, telling himself he wouldn't be there long enough to bother sitting down. He promised himself that when his feet touched the ground he'd be off, out the door and headed for home.

Before he had a chance to carry out his plan, he got waylaid by the smallest policeman he'd ever seen, or at least he thought must be a cop, this being a cops-only bar. The little man wasn't in uniform but on closer inspection had a badge sticking out of his suit coat pocket, evidently just shoved there when leaving the precinct. Humph also noticed in the second before the man spoke that he must indeed be a cop because his presence drew no particular attention.

"Benjamin Arlington," the man said, extending his hand. Humph started to present himself in turn but the man said, "No need, Humphrey. I know who you are."

The man's eyes seemed amiable enough so Humph told him to just call him Humph.

They drank in silence for a few minutes, Humph regarding him through the mirror behind the bar. There was enough space between the whiskies and gins and vodkas on the shelf in front of the mirror that allowed Humph to do so. Had the bottles been lined up next to each other the little man's face would not have been visible. He was too short for his face to be seen above them.

Humph had to lean slightly forward to hear the detective when he finally spoke after their handshake.

"I am aware of the investigation into Madden and friends. I was included because I have known Owney Madden most of my life. I've never been able to crucify him for any of his sins but I've come close. I grew up in

Hell's Kitchen where Madden became a man to be feared even before he started shaving. The story goes that he'd killed six men by then. I sometimes think, looking back on those years, that I became a cop because I was too small to be of any use to Madden and his gang of toughs. Life is ironic at times, would you not agree, Humph?"

"And I became too big to be much of anything else than a cop. I was kept studying too much to be spending idle time in the street."

"Another?" asked the detective.

Humph didn't answer. He posed a question of his own while the detective signaled for refills.

"I assume you have questions about the case. Or have you made progress of some kind that you want to tell me about. I have made progress, as of today in fact, or rather your surprisingly efficient Women's Bureau has."

"We have a women's bureau? I had no idea."

"It's been around for more than 20 years," said Humph. "I hadn't heard of it either."

Humph quickly explained the Eve part of the equation.

"We haven't rescued her yet but that's being worked on. She's my stepdaughter but the women's bureau who tracked her down doesn't want me to ride in on a white horse and gum up the works. So I'm here, drinking with you."

"That's wonderful news, Humph, and you've told me something else I didn't know. As the crow flies, headquarters and this precinct are less than a mile apart but communication is too long a word for some people to deal with."

"What have you got?" Humph demanded, suddenly impatient with the anecdotal tone.

"Simply put, Humph, all I've got personally is that Madden has somehow sensed that the heat is on. He has left the city for the pastoral pleasures of Arkansas. He's not hiding. The locals have all welcomed him and his squad of…what shall I call these henchmen? Counsellors. I guess that will do. He's ensconced in the town's best hotel with 24-hour room service."

"What about his trucking services and their trips to Montreal? And for that matter, what have your boys learned about Madden's relationship with the esteemed broker, Mr. Reginald Ostenbruch?"

"We have nothing that will doom either one, Humph, but we have made a further connection between the two. Several months ago, the two dined at The Ritz here in New York. No one can claim to have overheard their conversation but their two waiters agree that snippets such as 'Nowhere but up' and 'A marriage made in heaven' were spoken. The meal lasted a good three hours, which means they were undoubtedly drinking the best tea The Ritz had to offer. Just the choice of such a hotel speaks volumes because Owney is still an Irish farm boy when push comes to shove."

The detective emphasized that confirmation of such meetings carries weight in court.

"What about all those buildings he owns, according to City Hall?"

"We've verified a number of them. They are either speaks or warehouses with laughable signs such as 'Maternity Wear Imports'."

The detective went on to say that his men had watched deliveries being made to some of the warehouses. Whatever they're unloading, it weighs a lot more than frilly things for pregnant women.

"It'll take us a good while, Humph, but we'll document as many warehouses as we can find from that list."

Humph was satisfied.

"One last question, detective. Do all roads lead to Montreal?"

The detective laughed.

"Not quite, Humph. Some do for sure but the majority take us to our very own East Coast port cities, from the Carolinas to Massachusetts to Maine."

"Do the ones that lead to Montreal testify to any kind of involvement by a certain pillar of society named Randall Overton?"

The little detective took a sip of his drink while Humph finished his. The detective apparently possessed one of an investigator's most important characteristics. He was profoundly patient. Humph thought he had mastered patience but this case was too personal.

"We have made discreet inquiries, Humph, but the chief of detectives, who at first wanted no part in such an investigation, declared a state of eggshells for anyone pursing this line of investigation. So our progress can't really be called progress. But thanks to an acquaintance of yours, your client in fact, who, as a son is a reliable witness, we know first of all that Mr. Overton has a mistress in Montreal. The city apparently abounds in ready mistresses well able to ingratiate themselves in high society on the arms of a gentleman of means. Mr. Overton's mistress, by all accounts, makes Parisian sexual fantasies seem tame.

"Overton is discreet but it is easier to bribe bellboys and waiters in Montreal than here in New York, not that we're reticent about accepting gratuities for services rendered. Some of our sources pretended to speak only French but we were quickly able to find Montreal cops willing to translate for a fee."

In short, the detective said, Overton thinks himself such a big shot that he makes no effort to conceal his business endeavors in Montreal.

"He looks down on Canadians, not all, but certainly the French courtesans. They don't have a British lineage. However, he clearly approves of their way of spicing up his existence. He is circumspect in the extreme in New York but utterly careless in Montreal."

In short, the detective said, the son's evidence was priceless.

"We even managed to follow him to the head office of the distillery in question. We don't know what was discussed but considering Mr. Overton's other enterprises there was no discernable reason for him to visit this place, other than the fact he is a majority shareholder. The meeting lasted more than an hour. As in the case of the broker and the gangster at the Ritz in New York, we have a solid connection. What we need now is a manifest showing what his trucks delivered to New York. We're still investigating."

Humph was suddenly in heaven. The news about Eve had left him floating in space. These connections went up to Heaven itself. There was indeed hope.

Humph walked home. It was a good distance. When he felt emotional, he preferred to think while moving. Emotionality was a state of being he generally avoided. Such contemplations, the seated ones, never ended well.

CHAPTER 18

THE next day he went looking for Duff. For some reason, Humph felt he needed corroboration from a cop he knew.

Duff was sitting on the stoop when Humph arrived. His eyes were open but he seemed asleep somehow. Humph didn't say a word. He sat beside him.

A big truck suddenly slammed on the brakes. The tires screeched and the vehicle ended up diagonally across the street. That elicited more horn-honking than Duff could bear. He threw a beer bottle at the truck.

"What's got you so down?" Humph asked.

"What? Can't hear you! Inside! Let's go inside."

Duffy plunked himself down on his sofa, wedging himself into the corner so he wouldn't have to expend any effort sitting up straight.

"Talk," Humph said.

Duffy reminded Humph about the girl who shared a taxi with him after his evening of researching a speak in the Bronx.

"Remember?"

"Yes."

"Well, she decamped yesterday. She had been staying here and I thought we were as happy as pigs, you know? I couldn't believe my eyes when I saw her backside descending my steps to the sidewalk. I thought we worked together pretty well in all matters."

"What matters?" asked Humph.

"Well, the couple kind of matter and the investigative one."

Humph still looked perplexed.

"The speakeasy investigation. In particular, the Eve angle."

"The Bronx broad was happy at first. 'Being a cop, what a fun job,' she said. We tried to hit two speaks a night, no more because I've been on day shift since you started this whole missing-person thing with brokers and assorted bad guys."

"I appreciate the unpaid overtime you were putting in," said Humph in a tone that Duffy wasn't quite sure was sincere.

"She said Eve was the only girl I ever talked about, night after night. In no uncertain terms, I reminded her who Eve was and why we had to find her. Then, all of a sudden, two nights ago at a place way up in Washington Heights, she turns on me.

'What's this filly Eve got going with you? Am I your girl or not?' We hardly said a word to each on the way home. When we got here I headed straight for the bed but she didn't come. 'Are you in the washroom?' I yell out. She shouts back, 'No, I ain't!' Finally, I get up and go to the living room. There she is, right here where I'm sitting now, still dressed. She announces that when the sun comes up she's history. Thinking she had too much to drink, I ignored her and went back to bed. When I got up this morning, she was gone."

Humph commiserated for a few minutes before standing up to make sure he had Duff's attention.

"We've found Eve. We still have to extricate her from whatever son of a bitch is holding her but we know where she is. The gals in the Women's Bureau called me in and told me all about it. They told me to sit tight because they didn't want my emotions to blow up their efforts. I think they're trying to get together enough bodies, men, too, to waltz into the speak and rescue her."

Duffy's mouth dropped open.

"That's deadly, Humph!"

Humph was taken aback. "Deadly?"

"Great. It means great. Keep forgetting you're not Irish. You could pass as one of us if you'd learn to talk. Anyway, back to what you were saying about young Eve."

"Well, there's not much more than that simple fact plus the fact that I'm under orders to sit on my keester till further notice."

"No one," said Duffy with the hint of a twinkle in his left eye, "has told me to keester myself."

At first, Humph was grateful for Duffy's enthusiasm. Then images of an Irish bull in a china shop invaded his mind. He shut down his alarm by pondering why he often focused on just one of a person's eyes when listening. He had noticed the twinkle in Duffy's left eye because that eye was the more animated. It even seemed to be backlit. Did one of his eyes do that?

"Forget it Duffy. Keep your nose out of the business of rescuing Eve. The police ladies are all over it. I even met the one who determined Eve was in the speak she was investigating. She's clearly a fine officer by any standard, Duffy. Keep your keester far away from that speak."

WAYNE CLARK | One Murder Too Many

"Truth be told, Humph, I've got an out-of-town assignment coming up in two days so I can't be gallivanting and getting zozzled as the young people say." He said no more, hoping to aggravate Humph for fun. But Humph didn't bite. He was still standing. His arms were folded across his chest. His eyes bore into the Irishman.

"You used to be fun, Humph. You should take up serious drinking again and be yourself."

Humph continued to stare at him.

"You're really some dry shite, Humph. OK, I'll tell you. I'm being sent to Montreal. Thanks to your talebearer, Edna was it?"

"Edith."

"Yes, Edith. Thanks to her we have a weighty list of trucking companies owned by people of interest to us, none other than the likes of Owney Madden and Reginald Ostenbruch and possibly others. One assumes the trucks were registered to them, or a company they probably own. I want to chat up our Montreal opposites to see what they know."

Humph said that was excellent news.

"Let's keep tightening the noose on those bastards."

"Couldn't have said it better, Humph. I just hope I don't have to devote myself to business for my entire stay. I want to brush up on my *parlez-vous*, you know."

Humph finally smiled at his incorrigible friend.

"Are you going to get a phone, Duffy?"

"What on earth does that have to do with Montreal?"

"Well, Duffy, I decided to join the moderns some time ago. It's not likely I'll ever find myself with a flapper girl but now, like her, I have my own telephone. This case we're working on, it has so many threads. You know, my original client up in the Bronx. And his dad, who's now kind of a suspect in the bootlegging business. Then there's the Women's Bureau, which is probably tired of sending Western Union messengers to my place, let alone kid police officers who should be doing something more important. There's Edith. There's the broker. Who knows, Owney Madden might be partial to phones as well."

"You only wanted it to be able to jabber with Edith. I know you."

Humph smiled because there might have been a touch of truth in what he said.

"Anyway, I have one of my own. What got me thinking about it was last year. Remember reading the big headlines about a telephone cable being laid underneath the damned ocean itself and a phone call being made from London to New York? Our beloved constitution isn't the only thing to have changed in this decade."

Duffy's face revealed confusion.

"What bloody change?"

"The fucking 18th Amendment to our constitution. The denial of our right to enjoy drinking establishments. Christ, Duffy, I would have thought you'd even have a tattoo like a sailor's tattoo, something like a skull and crossbones and a bloodied number 18."

It was Duffy's turn to laugh.

"I don't have a tattoo but that, sir, is going to change. That amendment thing is going to bleed all over my arm."

CHAPTER 19

THE next morning, Humph called Frankie before finishing his morning coffee.

In their last meeting, at New York's oldest private club, the Union Club on Fifth, Frankie appeared to have fully matured. Confronted now by the same "new Frankie", Humph wondered whether the Eureka moment had been Frankie realizing that he had no obligation to his distant, condescending, emotionless father. Perhaps Frankie finally understood that the bastard was not someone he should strive to please. Humph wasn't sure because he didn't know his real father but his stepfather was always on his side in life, in the ultimately petty disputes of childhood and the life-defining ones of his later teens when he had to decide between his family's values and the unbearably tangible temptations placed before him every day by Five Points gangs. Many of them were his schoolmates, guys he liked, guys he'd defend on the school grounds. Deciding wasn't easy. Deep down inside, he knew they were good people. They weren't trying to trap him. They were just offering opportunities, as friends, as former school buddies.

Humph's father never said they were evil. He just somehow made Humph understand that they were thinking their lives were all about today.

"Our lives," his father would say, "are about the countless days that follow, about leaving every possibility open and on the table, possibilities that a young man can't begin to imagine. You have to believe me. I have lived that truth as has your mother."

Some days his father would ask him why so many old people, men and women, looked peaceful despite their poverty, their crippling age and physical pains.

His parents succeeded as parents. Humph was never again tempted by easy money or power. To him, becoming a cop was deciding to be of service. It was only later that he learned that being honest was one of the most difficult things in life. The odds, at least in New York, were heavily against you. Most of the people he got to know as a young man talked about survival, not honesty.

When Frankie answered, Humph interrupted his "Hello" to say he had a phone again but the number was different. "Take down my number. Call me day or night."

"I'm impressed," Frankie said. "I took you for a stuck-in-the-mudder. No offense."

His laughter made Humph realize the dig was deserved.

"I've got news, Humph. I got fired by CBS. They said I seemed incapable of writing stuff that was true to the original storyline. Maybe they were right."

"Not sure what you mean, Frankie," said Humph.

"Let's just say that their characters walked a straight line. My mind doesn't work that way. I started thinking that the only fiction I should be writing is my fiction. My characters, my realities, my possibilities."

Humph said he understood that. He was about to say that he was a big reader of fiction but decided not to. His nature was not part of the investigation.

Frankie then announced he was writing his own stories.

"I'm doing a story right now for *True Manhattan Detective* magazine. They have a huge circulation. If they accept it I'm on the high road."

Humph didn't reply for a minute at least. Frankie kept saying, "You still there, Humph. You still there?"

"Yeah, sorry Frankie. I was just thinking. I'm not a fast as you when it comes to thinking. But what I ended up with was a question. Here it is. Stories in True Manhattan Detective, which I read, are supposed to be true, factual, verifiable, solid, reliable, beyond question. So, what I'm asking, Frankie, is where in the hell does your fiction enter the picture?"

Frankie immediately said Humph had misunderstood.

"I was just saying that I'm my own man now. I make my living as a writer and I write what interests me. I hope someone shows my byline to Dad someday. I'd sure love to be a fly on the wall for that moment."

Frankie added that what he wrote for *True Manhattan Detective* was true.

"It's just that it's me who decides what cases to write about, not like at CBS where I had to be true to their characters. Understand?"

He added that Humph was wrong in thinking that *True Manhattan Detective* published only true stories.

"When I first approached them last year they said what they were looking for was what they called mystery fiction. Apparently, that's what sold at first. I loved the category. I'd never heard of it before. Then they told me this year that non-fiction stories were now selling better. At first I said 'shit' but then when I met you, I figured you'd be a great source of real information."

Humph had to smile. At the start of this case, the stock humiliation, Humph felt he probably wouldn't be able to do much for Frankie. Then when that led to the disreputable broker and finally to gangland bootlegging, Humph valued Frankie as a source of information, particularly about his own father. Now, Humph realized, Frankie was using him. Humph instantly shed any guilt he'd felt for taking Frankie's money even though he didn't believe he could do a damn thing for him.

"Hope you don't mind, Humph, you know, me using you this way."

Humph's smile turned into a little laugh.

"Not at all, Frankie. Not one bit. I truly hope to see what you end up saying about this case. It's a doozy."

Frankie sounded thrilled, as if he'd been given permission to plagiarize another man's mind and use the pickings in a story he could sell.

Then Humph let a little air out of Frankie's balloon.

"I'm going to write about the case as well," he announced. "For the *New York World*."

"When?" The alarm in Frankie's voice was apparent.

"When we have enough information to start laying charges. Writing about the case now would just send the guilty parties into hiding and looking for ways to cover up their connection with the bootlegging and the kidnapping of Eve."

Humph pressed the receiver firmly against his ear. He was sure he heard the wheel's turning in Frankie's mind.

"Do you think that will be soon, Humph?"

"Can't say yet. But things are just starting to fall into place."

"What things?"

"Can't tell you yet."

Humph heard Frankie's sigh race through the phone line, all the way from the Bronx to Chinatown. Humph suddenly loved his phone.

"I thought I'd have an exclusive," Frankie said with a much smaller voice than before.

Humph didn't want to entirely deflate the kid's dreams. To save the day, he reminded Frankie that it would take *True Manhattan Detective* too long to hit the newsstands to actually break such a big story.

"But what you'd have, Frankie, would be all the exclusive, day-in and day-out details of how the case was cracked. You'd be taking your readers on a walk in my shoes."

Frankie was silent for so long Humph rose his voice.

"Are you still there. Frankie? Can you hear me?"

"Yeah, yeah, Humph. I was just thinking about what you said. I guess what you said makes sense. That bit about people walking in your shoes thanks to my story, I can see that. I think the magazine will love it because when you lay your charges the whole city will be eating up the story. So, do we have a deal, Humph?"

"I guess," said Humph, "there's no way to actually shake hands on a telephone. Tell you what, write me a letter outlining our basic arrangement and I'll sign it and return it to you. You'd have something to show your editors when you pitch the story. Is that the term you guys use, pitching a story?"

Frankie was delighted.

"Can't tell you how much I'm in your debt. Speaking of debt, yours not mine, I imagine, send me another bill for services rendered. OK?"

Now it was Humph's turned to feel energized. His finances had sunk precipitously without other paying clients since meeting Frankie, or more accurately since Eve was kidnapped. She became his sole priority. Just last week he was so concerned about money he had even debated going phoneless again to avoid having to pay the three-dollar-a-month phone bill. A few days later when the Women's Bureau called he realized the phone bill was small in the scheme of things.

Humph's second phone call was to Gerald Franklin at the *World*. He had to look up the number in his homemade phone book, a piece of cardboard cut out from a box of breakfast cereal. So far, he'd collected five numbers: Frankie, his client, Gerald Franklin at the paper, Colin Lenester on Park Avenue, Captain Connolly at the Women's Bureau, and Edith's work number. On the other side of the piece of cardboard was the name of the cereal, Armour's Toasted Corn Flakes. The box promised, "You'll like the taste." And he did but he was always puzzled by the boast that the cereal was "carefully packaged at our modern sunlit plant." How, Humph wondered every morning as he read and re-read the box, could sunlight improve the taste of a processed product?

Before dialing the newspaperman's number, Humph found a pencil stub and scribbled a note to himself on his phone list reminding him to buy a proper notebook for the numbers. Who knows how many numbers he'd have a year from now? He was feeling strangely organized, which his mind appreciated, and looking forward to an inclement day when he could reach someone without having to freeze or get soaking wet in the process.

He was immediately put through to Gerald Franklin at the *New York World*

"Just wanted to let you know I got my phone back."

"You absolutely need one in this business," said Gerald. "If your story, or should I say stories, look promising enough I could have probably talked the paper into paying for your phone."

"So much for impetuous me."

Gerald laughed.

"That's the last word I would ever have chosen to describe you, Humph."

"Me too."

"So," Gerald said, getting serious again. "You've got news?"

"No arrests, no warrants issued. In short, nothing for publication. But I'm hoping that Eve will be rescued in the coming days. The cops are also expanding their bootlegging investigation to Montreal. But I can't give you names yet."

"Sounding good, Humph. Sounding good."

"Which brings me," Humph said, "to one of the reasons I'm calling. When it comes time to write all this, how do we go about it? I have to be up front. I don't type."

"Of course not," said Gerald with a chuckle. "Your fingers are too big for any keyboard known to man. But they can hold a pen, can't they."

"Yeah, I guess that's one way of getting the story to you. But, damn, that will take a long time. This story could be big. I was hoping you'd say I could dictate it to one of your secretaries."

"Or," said Gerald, "since you don't have writing experience, for the first stories at least, you could dictate them to another reporter. A lot of them know shorthand. I'd pick a crime reporter and he'd actually rewrite what you dictate as his own story. But you'd get the major byline, don't worry."

They chatted about a few other aspects of reporting before Gerald said he had to get to a story meeting. "I'm keeping my fingers crossed for Eve," he said before hanging up.

Humph then called the broker's office and asked to speak to Edith.

"Who shall I say is calling?" the woman's voice asked hesitantly.

"Just tell her it's Humph. She knows me."

"Can you wait a moment, sir?" the woman said. A few seconds later, he could hear several voices in the distance.

A man's voice came on the line.

"Sir, there's been a terrible incident. I'm afraid to have to tell you that Edith is now deceased."

Humph leapt to his feet and was about to shout that jokes like that are not funny, you son of a bitch. He stopped himself when the man's voice said everyone at the office was so distraught they were going to ask Mr. Ostenbruch if they could close the office for a day in memoriam.

Humph willed himself to stay calm.

"What happened ?"

The man explained that she was found on the sidewalk in front of a tea salon near the office. After a pause that was unbearable to Humph, the man said her throat had been cut.

"I have the name of the detective who is investigating. I don't know any other details. I'm so sorry, sir."

Humph was about to phone the police station, then thought better of it. He needed answers right away and his physical presence was sufficient to get them faster in person. The desk sergeant was the same one Humph reported to in his days on the force. The guy appreciated bluntness.

On the way to the station, one young man and a middle-aged woman swore almost poetically at Humph after he'd accidentally bumped them out of his way while hurrying up the Bowery, blind to anything in front of him. By the time he arrived at the stationhouse, he knew what his questions, or rather demands, would be: 1) Who, if anyone, has been identified as a suspect? and 2) Was Edith in possession of any papers connected with the brokerage?, and 3) Was Officer Duffy aware of the murder?

The desk sergeant's answers were quick in coming.

"We haven't a clue who might be responsible for her murder, and even if we did, I wouldn't tell you, Humph. You're not on the force.

"Secondly, Sgt. Bosco…"

Humph interrupted:

"Billy Bosco, late of Missouri?"

"One and the same," said the sergeant. "Now if you're finished interrupting me, yes, he found documents. But he didn't share their import with lowly me. And as for your last question, our dear buddy and bootlegger Officer Duffy is undoubtedly honorably representing the NYPD in one of those little bistro places in Montreal."

Humph's first question was whether the sarge had a number for Duffy's hotel. He did. The second question was when and where could he find Billy Bosco. The answer wasn't a surprise.

This would be a drinking night, Humph decided as he walked down the precinct stationhouse steps and turned left toward the bar that gave birth to the nickname he hated as a cop, Officer Barstool.

Humph found Bosco alone at a table. Humph preferred the bar because the stools were high enough for his legs to dangle comfortably.

Bosco was friendly enough, if Humph remembered correctly, but he tended to apply Missouri instincts a little too predictably. He liked New York, he once said, because the city wanted to send immigrants back where they came from.

"Ain't that many foreigners back home," he'd frequently point out with something close to pride. However, he got along well with most of the guys on the force because he didn't include the Irish among the foreigners. "We got'em back home, too."

But, Humph remembered that, on seeing his squat body and balding head, he wasn't stupid.

"Hey, Bosco," Humph said as if there were old friends. "Mind if I join you?" It was Sunny who once told Humph that he had acting talent. She would jokingly say they should share a burlesque stage someday. She explained that Humph the giant plodded physically. His motions were deliberate and steady. And his words were few for the most part. However, Sunny said there were other moments when he became absolutely animated. Those moments were so few that she said they were as if he had become possessed. Sunny said actors want to be possessed by their characters. Humph wasn't sure he understood what she was saying but he was warmed by the thought that his love saw things in him others didn't.

When he greeted Bosco, it was his Sunny persona doing so. It was only after pulling out a chair and sitting that he had the flash realization that Sunny was by his shoulder. Despite the shock of Edith's murder, he felt a cocoon of purpose that shut out the despair. Until his walk from home, he hadn't realized how deep the wound was. He had never articulated for himself his feelings about Edith, let alone imagine a future with her. Now he realized some part of him had done all that wordlessly.

Bosco seemed happy to have company or was it just Southern hospitality. Didn't matter, decided Humph.

"Papers, Bosco. You recovered some?"

"Sure did but I can't make head nor tail of them."

"I think I can help. In another case, I got to know the victim well. She had been of immense help in an investigation of bootlegging and kidnapping. Patrolman Duffy has been assigned to the case. This is far more than a murder, Bosco. It's all tangled up in a gangland hell of prostitutes, speaks, bootlegging, name it. Duffy's got the lead because of information Edith handed over to me originally. The tentacles of this mess go everywhere, Bosco. At this very moment, Duffy is in Montreal trying to build our case. You know we don't do that very often."

"Indeed we don't," said Bosco. "Why in the hell is a bloody patrolman acting like a detective?"

Humph laughed and ordered a bourbon.

"I was amazed as well when that happened but because the investigation is basically based on a case I've made, and one in which Duffy has assisted greatly on his own time, and the fact I'm no longer on the force, I couldn't very well object. Duffy's tenacity is…well, let's say, myself having a personal stake in the case, let's say his tenacity is my one and only hope of seeing justice done. The department knows that, too, but regs being regs, they can't make his role as detective official at the moment."

Bosco started nodding, and as his mind digested the argument, kept nodding.

"So what you're saying, Humph, is that my case, the murder of this office worker, Edith, is an appendage—we don't use that word where I'm from, learned it here—of a major investigation."

"Exactly," said Humph. "No one, least of all me, wants to steal your case, Bosco. But because, like Duffy, I'm so invested in it, I need to know everything. In the end, I might even be able to come up with, maybe not the murderer, but the person who ordered it. You'd probably even get a promotion if you solved that detail."

Bosco beamed.

"I need something like that to establish my boner fightees here, you know what I mean?"

"Very well, indeed," said Humph, reassuring the detective that his bona fides would be clearly established.

After two more rounds, paid for by Bosco, the two headed back to the precinct station. Bosco led the way to the second floor and the detective division offices. After a moment of half-drunken rummaging, he pulled out a file folder.

"These are the papers the victim carried. I think they weren't stolen because she'd been carrying them in her hand and after the bastard came up behind her and slit her throat, they fell to the pavement and she fell on top of them."

The bourbons allowed Humph to bear the cruel details of Edith's end. He grabbed the folder and clasped Bosco's shoulder. No words of thanks were necessary.

CHAPTER 20

THE call came just after midnight. Humph had just finished reading the papers Edith had on her when she was murdered. They confirmed that Madden and the broker had been doing business together.

The call was from the Women's Bureau of the NYPD. They had Humph's number because he had been calling two or three times a day for news about Eve. They kept telling him he'd be the first to know when they had news. At last, they had news.

On the other end was Karena Melchinskaya, the young officer who'd tracked down Eve's whereabouts. From the start, Humph had feared the task would be an impossible one considering the countless speakeasies in the city.

"Humph! We've got your girl. She's no worse for wear, just angry as I won't say what."

"Where is she now? I need to be with her."

"The feeling's mutual," said Karena, who sounded as excited as Humph. "As soon as we got her in the patrol car outside the club she said, 'Take me to Humph.' Then she took a deep breath and started to cry."

"For God's sake, bring her here, Karena. You can get here faster than I can get to the station."

"Of course, we could do that but there's something you've got to think about first. Bear with me here, Humph. I've been giving this a lot of thought."

Karena then explained why Eve shouldn't go either to her old apartment or to Humph's.

"The people we arrested tonight at the speak aren't the actual people behind the kidnapping. They just work for them. They're being grilled right now for names of the instigators. You were the one who told us it could have been the mob. The names of guys like that don't come out easily. That's why I think we got to be a secretive as they are. Follow me, Humph?"

Humph's mind was racing like a Stakes winner at Belmont in Queens.

"But where?" he asked.

"There are two options that I can see, Humph. One is in a jail cell with all the comforts of home added, or... Or she can stay with me. I live on Jackson Street. Eve can have the sofa."

"Jackson?," said Humph. "You're close by. I'm on Henry Street."

"It will take you no time with those long legs of yours, Humph."

Humph laughed, more in relief than at the pleasant familiarity of Karena's teasing.

When Humph first met her at the Bureau she was all business, the way young people are in the company of an unsmiling older boss. He liked the Karena he was hearing on the phone. It was enough to make him say yes to her proposal.

"Wonderful. Humph. I can take her home now. Do you want to meet us here at the station or at my place?"

"At the station!"

On his way out the door he grabbed the photo of Eve's mom. It would keep her company, he figured, until the nightmare vanished.

Forty minutes later, the three of them, Humph, Eve and Karena, rode a taxi to Jackson Street. Eve and Karena were in the back seat, where Humph wouldn't fit without angling his feet to the other side of the vehicle. At the station, Eve threw herself into Humph's arms and wouldn't let go until after he picked her up in a bear hug and walked down the precinct steps with her still in his arms. They said little in the cab beyond Humph saying, "I can't believe you're free" and the gutsy Eve echoing, "Ha. You can't believe it. How do you think I feel?" To Humph, the soft laughter felt like a happy dream.

Karena's place was smaller than Humph's but cozier and more comfortable. On the wall opposite the door was a large painting of wheat fields.

"Makes me feel at home in Ukraine," Karena said. "Wheat fields as far as the eye can see."

Two easy chairs faced the sofa, which was under the east-facing window.

"I get the morning sun, which I like," said Karena, "except when I'm working nights. It will rise far too early tomorrow."

"And I won't give a damn," said Eve as she did a quick pirouette in front of the sofa.

Karena returned from the kitchen with an unopened bottle of vodka. She was beaming, Humph noticed. This was probably the biggest case she had ever broken and would bode well for the rest of her career. But Humph also thought part of it was her evident liking for Eve.

Humph raised his hand to decline the vodka a moment later.

"You girls go ahead. Before I join you, I need to know what you discovered, Karena. Everything about tonight and leading up to it."

When she finished describing the rescue, Eve rose from the sofa and, standing behind Karena's chair, reached down and hugged her with her head pressed against the policewoman's face. Clearly, they'd hit it off, thought Humph. He was pleased because he had good feelings about Karena, too. Karena reached back and touched Eve's cheek for a brief moment. To break the embrace, Karena said,

"In my home country we'd be dancing like fools by now."

Eve replied, looking sad all of a sudden:

"Dancing is no longer my favorite word. Dancing on demand for fucking Madden's guys..." She didn't finish. Karena and Humph got the point.

"Let's hope that someday the joy comes back, Eve. You've danced since you were a kid."

She led Humph from his chair and onto the sofa. She cuddled next to him.

Karena said they got their break when two goons entered the bar from the hallway at the back and started to lead Eve to the door. To Karena's astonishment, her drunk actor-companion hurried out the door ahead of them. Karena followed them, only steps behind. On the sidewalk, one of the gangsters stepped to the curb and raised his hand for a cab. A taxi appeared almost instantly. Before it braked to a full stop, the actor pushed the goon hard. He fell in front of the cab, yelling at the impact of bumper and pavement. That gave Karena enough time to land a blow of her blackjack on the other gangster's head.

"You should have seen her, Humph!" said Eve. "I was squirming like mad trying to break this goon's grip when I saw Karena from the corner of my eye. Her face was as calm as if she were sprinkling pepper on her morning eggs except that she had raised her club, which she had carried in her purse, as high as she could and with only the slightest pause brought it down with such force on his head that I swear her legs left the pavement. Lights out. I was free!"

Karena explained that the gesture was like cutting off a chicken's head. "You make sure you swing hard enough to chop it off completely in one try."

As the goon dropped to the pavement, Karena sent the actor back inside the bar to phone for police backup. Karena's gangster was out cold. The other one lay moaning in front of the cab. The cabbie was pleading that it wasn't his fault. "The guy there, he came out of nowhere, lady." Karena corrected him. "It's officer, not lady. By the way, you deserve a medal." The cabbie looked thoroughly confused. Finally, he figured things out and smiled. "Yes, sir, officer."

When the actor returned to the street, he had a full glass in his hand.

"Backup's on the way."

Karena poured Humph a drink and refilled Eve's.

"Night after night of staking out a place and sipping your drink while your partner inhales glass after glass, well, it's sleep-inducing," Karena said. "I suspect the force of my blow to the guy's head reflected the boredom. Bopping him was liberating for me and Eve."

"I wish I'd been there to see it and applaud," said Humph.

"All that was left," said Karena, "was to sweat them to find out who owns that speak and the extent of their operation. And most importantly, who ordered Eve's abduction."

Humph raised his glass.

"To a great piece of police work. Cheers."

Eve explained that she was actually walking from her place to Humph's when a car pulled up about 20 feet ahead of her. She had no reason to pay any attention. The car had stopped in front of a Polish sausage-maker's place. As soon as she approached the car, its driver's side door opened suddenly and all but blocked the sidewalk. The passenger had exited the car and was a step behind her. He grabbed her first, then the driver joined in, pushing Eve into the back seat. The other goon got in beside her. The whole thing took barely 30 seconds, Eve said.

"From there I was taken to a brothel on 6th Street on the West Side. I was shut in a closet on the second floor. I could hear girls talking and sometimes being ordered to shut up and go to their rooms. 'Time to earn your keep,' said a man. Finally, a big guy took me out of the closet, threw me over his shoulder and took me out the back way. A fancy car was waiting. I was gagged and thrown in the back seat. Half an hour later, the big guy threw me over his shoulder again and carried me up a fire escape. On the third landing, they put me down and shoved me through an open door, which they locked once we were all in. After a long wait, someone who called himself the manager of the joint told me that from now on I'd be dancing for his customers, whoever they were.

"I didn't know where I was at that time. I heard him say to someone, 'Who knows, the kid might have what it takes to become my star attraction. What more could you ask for? When opportunity knocks, you know the rest.' They let me cool off for the next couple of days. They tried to make nice but it was clear there was no chance of escape. And so it began."

As the sun started to rise, little vodka remained in the bottle. Karena promised to let Humph know as soon as they'd finished their questioning of the two goons.

Eve had already fallen asleep on Humph's shoulder. With Karena's help, he extricated himself. At the door he gave Karena a smile.

"Thank you, Officer Melchinskaya."

"You pronounced that very well. I'm thinking of having my family named changed or at least shortened."

"Don't," said Humph. Not having known his birth family, he felt having a name that truly belonged to you was too valuable to part with.

On his way home he wondered why it mattered. He didn't know but it did.

CHAPTER 21

TWO days later, Humph was awakened just after 7 o'clock by banging on his door. Before opening it, he could hear his neighbors in the hallway complaining about the racket.

At the door was none other than Duffy. Who else would act like he was banging down a suspect's door?

Humph let him in and, once Duffy had sat at the big table, Humph said, "Shut up." It was becoming Humph's standard morning greeting.

Duffy obeyed while Humph prepared coffee and, huffing and puffing with annoyance, got himself dressed.

Once Humph plunked down two coffees and sat, Duffy said:

"Montreal says hello, Humph."

"I don't know a soul there for Christ's sake.

Never been."

"Well, Humph, you've got a treat in store. They say hi to anyone and everyone. That town is dedicated to fun around the clock. Ooh-la-la, as they say."

Humph said he'd had occasion to talk to Duffy's sergeant.

"He said you were undoubtedly knee-deep in the pleasures to be had at the city's bistros. It sounded a touch too Parisian to believe, especially knowing you."

"A dead-on deduction, Humph. Bistros are for tourists from Arkansas, not worldly New Yorkers."

"Spare me the details, Duffy. What did you learn?"

"What did I learn? Let me think about that a minute. Yes, yes. The first thing I learned was that French was easy to learn. And that for the simple reason that the people who matter in this world, doormen, maître d's and the young women behind said doors, parley American, or at least enough American to keep a smile on your face."

Humph was now up and again pacing around the table with his coffee in hand.

"It's not even eight o'clock but I must tell you to shut up for the second time this morning. First of all, my girl is now safe and sound, thanks to a pretty remarkable gal in the Women's Bureau. She rescued Eve from a speak where she had been imprisoned as a dancer and I won't say what else by guys who just have to be mobbed up. They're still under interrogation so I don't know where we stand as far as getting to the bottom of things. But know this, Duffy, my world has changed since we last saw each other. I'm happy but know that I'm in no god-damned mood for anecdotes about the girls who decorate starry nights in Montreal."

Duffy pulled a flask from his pocket and emboldened his coffee.

After a lengthy swig of his coffee, he came clean.

"I made progress. Nothin' definitive, as the lawyers say,

but progress. I went to the big distillery up there. They try to put me off by saying they ship their product all over the world. I finally got them to admit that they have a good customer in New York but they have no idea where he shipped his purchases. I pressed a little harder and learned that the client's name was Overton, but not Randall Overton, the man we suspect. The name on the account was none other than young Frankie, the son."

Duffy couldn't believe his ears.

"There's no bloody way the kid is involved. His old man uses lawyers to keep him at arm's length times 100. The kid can't fart without permission from one of his father's lawyers."

"I know he's your client, Humph, but keep your bloody eyes open to all possibilities. It doesn't make sense to me either but paper doesn't always lie. They showed me the purchase orders."

Humph kept pacing but much more slowly. He was lost in thought.

"So you learned that and packed up to head home?"

"What do you take me for, you oversized leprechaun?"

Duffy then said he did what Humph would have done. He asked workers on the distillery's loading dock about certain shipments. He had the order numbers. The boys said they loaded the booze onto trucks with license plates from the province of Quebec.

"Then, like the detective I had better damn well become after this case, I investigated even further. I found out that Quebec plates resemble ours. Both New York and Quebec use yellow plates with black numbers and letters. I went back to the loading dock and asked the guys if they could have made a mistake. Absolutely not, they said. They had noticed something I didn't. They said that when they're standing on the dock looking down they can't always see the bottom of the plate. New York plates have 'NY' or 'New York' above the numbers. Quebec plates do the opposite. If a yellow plate has no numbers at the top, it's a

Quebec plate. 'Voilà, monsieur.'

"The next day, my instincts were mighty unhappy whilst I sampled my first whiskey of the day. I went to visit our counterparts in the Montreal police department. I'd heard from many casual discussions with locals that there was many a shady character hiding behind a badge in that city. That news made me feel right at home, Humph.

"However when I was finally ushered into the right detectives' playpen I found that they were acquitting themselves honorably indeed. They were able to tell me they had already had their suspicions, knowing very well the Prohibition nonsense in our country. Bootlegging was nothing new to them. What they'd learned after checking the Quebec plates used by, among others, our Frankie Overton, they discovered that all those plates were from trucks that had been reported stolen."

"I must say," Humph interrupted. "In my eyes at least, Duffy, you are restoring your reputation."

Duffy bowed his head and asked if Humph could refill his hip flask.

It was obvious, the Montreal cops agreed, that the shipper, whether Frankie or his high and mighty father, had local help in pulling off the switch of plates.

"Once the trucks left the distillery, with Quebec plates, they stopped somewhere and were reunited with U.S. plates for the trip home."

Humph had to agree it was a clever move on the part of both the distillery and the client, whoever he really was.

"I'm pleased to say that while some of the cops I dealt with were, on the one hand, French speaking, they confided after we got to know each other that they were Irish immigrants as well, although decades before. Said their bogger fathers married a French doll upon arriving here to dig some damn canal and they grew up as French as they were Irish. At least, they didn't grow up English."

"What's the term?" Humph said. "Oh yeah, you digress."

"Right you are, Humph. These fine men in Montreal blue went as far as to talk to their country's border cops. They asked them to pull over and have a chit chat with drivers of trucks with U.S. plates. Verify truck registrations, they were told. Find out who owns them, that sort of thing.

"It took a while, Humph, but their perseverance paid off. They learned that two trucking companies are involved in the New York-bound imports from our distillery. The owners are named Madden and Ostenbruch."

Duffy's silly smile of self-satisfaction was deservedly that of a Cheshire cat, a half drunken one.

Everything was connected, every suspicion. The most immediate task was to find out if your lad Frankie was the brainchild of the whole operation,"

As Duffy looked on, sipping excitedly from his flask, Humph picked up his new investigator's tool and phoned Frankie.

"Frankie, there are developments. I need to talk to you in person."

"Will I be able to write my story yet?"

"No. Still too early, Frankie, but what we have to talk about may change the direction of your story. When can we meet?"

"I'm going to Atlantic City tomorrow. I'll be there for three days, until the weekend."

"Can I meet you there?" Humph's tone was persistent,

"That would be awkward, Humph. I'll be accompanied by a young starlet from Hollywood. I'm hoping she'll never be out of my sight."

Humph realized he couldn't compete with a sexual assignation.

"Call me as soon as you return." Humph then made sure the kid had his number.

Humph hung up and turned to Duffy.

"Breakfast?"

"No way, my friend. Life's too good already. You got your Eve. I got my case made, or almost. Hell, Humph, I feel like catching the next train back to Montreal."

Humph realized his friend would go his own way today.

"I've got a lot to ponder," Humph finally said by way of an excuse for sidestepping a binge.

"*Bonne journée,*" said Duffy as he made his way out the door.

The days went by and Frankie didn't call. Humph was frustrated. Was he dealing with a criminal or a victim?

His spirits rose that afternoon when Eve called.

"Humph?"

"Yes. It's me, Eve. You OK?"

"To be honest, more than OK."

"Talk, talk, girl."

"Not sure how to tell you this but I talked to your client, Frankie."

"Today?" asked Humph.

Humph's voice was urgent.

"No. No. The other day. Last week."

"And?"

"He said he wanted to meet me. Said he wanted to write a story about me. He said that would be OK with you."

"How and earth did he find you? No one is supposed to know where you are."

"He must have called the Women's Bureau but it was Karena who asked me if I'd be willing to talk to Frankie. Remember, you had told her he was your client, that this whole affair started when you looked into his case."

Although what Eve said made sense, Humph didn't reply for at least a minute.

"Humph? Humph? You there?"

"Yeah. What did you tell him?"

"I said yes. And I met him. He's a dream, Humph. He's handsome, he's crazy rich, and he's sweet as can be."

"Did you go to his place?"

"No, no. We met at The Ritz. It was my first time there."

The fact that Frankie hadn't enticed her to his place was a relief but Humph still saw red flags all over the place.

"Where's the Eve I know and love? The cynical Eve? When you say sweet, how sweet?"

"Never met a guy like him," she said. "He was a perfect gentleman all evening."

Humph wasn't at peace with the idea of Eve dating Frankie.

"Eve, I know Frankie, but not as a person. I know him as a client. He's from another world than you or I."

"Well, to be honest, at this stage in my life I wouldn't mind a different world once in a while. Besides, what does that matter? He's just a guy. I used to meet guys from all sorts of backgrounds at the club. They're just people in the end."

"Exactly," agreed Humph. "And where did you meet the goddamned broker? He may very well have been the bastard who arranged your kidnapping."

Eve fell silent.

Humph waited. Getting no reply, he ventured:

"Can't you put him off for a while? Tell him you're busy the next time he calls. Tell him you've got things to figure out. Tell him you have a sick aunt in Florida?"

"I need someone to believe in, Humph. So far in my life everyone's been a shit."

As she said that her voice was breaking. She always used to be so tough, thought Humph. Realistic. Practical. The kidnapping has undone her, he thought. His little Eve. A survivor.

"Sorry, Eve," Humph said. "You know me. I suspect everyone. That's how a cop, and an ex-cop, is. Use your judgment but keep those beautiful eyes wide open. Promise?"

"Promise."

They hung up but Humph was far from reassured.

Humph had to wait the expected three days before Frankie called.

"What have you got for me, Humph?"

For some reason, Humph had hoped he would be man enough to start right by telling him he had drinks at The Ritz with Eve. He hadn't expected Frankie to actually ask permission. He wasn't proposing after all.

"I might have a few things you'll be interested in knowing. In return, Frankie, do you have anything for me?"

"What do you mean? You're the guy with all the information."

"And you're the guy who talked to Eve without talking to me first. Eve just told me you took her to The Ritz. You should have tried harder to get me."

"Sorry, Humph. I really need to start writing this story. It'll be my way of getting back at my father and the broker bastard."

Humph realized he had to accept Frankie's excuse. He also realized that if Eve liked him, she liked him. That simple. He would be wrong to deny her a new friend.

"OK, Frankie, let's meet at your place so we can have a good talk, and tell your butler guy to hold off on the drinks trolley until I say it's OK. I want us to understand each other perfectly."

"You're making me nervous, Humph."

"Good. Two days from now. Is 11 a.m. too early for you?"

Frankie laughed.

"That's the old me, Humph. I'm a working slug now."

It was Humph's turn to laugh.

He then phoned Karena's home. She told Humph the two guys they busted at the speakeasy had records going back a long time. She said that for the moment, they're going to be charged with running an establishment illegally selling spirits.

"Because there are thousands of people waiting to appear in court on Prohibition violations, it will be a good while before our two goons get to see a judge. The DA's office is trying to figure out a way of using their previous felonies as an excuse for detaining them without bail at the Tombs until trial."

"Smart," Humph said. "What if a big shot lawyer is granted a bail hearing and gets them out on some technicality or other?"

"That won't be a total loss," Karena said. "Just knowing who their lawyer is might tell us who their boss is, the one paying the legal fee."

"Got it," said Humph. "Is Eve there?"

"She's taking a nap but I'm going to wake her anyway. She needs you more than ever these days."

When Eve finally got to the phone, Humph popped his question.

"Hi, Eve. I'm going to Frankie's place on Thursday. We've got a lot to talk about. Do you want to join us?"

"God, yes. Thank you, thank you."

She sounded like a teenager for a second and that scared Humph. Did she have a childish infatuation with Frankie after one meeting. Over time, Humph began to think Frankie was probably a decent guy but as a spoiled rich kid whose father had no time for him he'd grown up with any toy he wanted. And when Humph recalled their first meeting, when a hungover Frankie was recounting how he loved throwing petting parties, he suspected that Frankie could easily be guilty of regarding people, especially attractive young woman, as toys. At least by having Eve in tow, Humph hoped Frankie would get the message that if he messed with Eve he messed with him, too.

When the day came, Humph picked up Eve at Karena's apartment on Jackson Street. The East River, only a couple of blocks away looked peaceful on this windless first day of August. As they walked up to Grand Street, Humph reined himself in so the walk would be leisurely enough to encourage conversation. By the time they were heading west on Grand on the way to a train to the Bronx, Humph had learned that Eve's on-and-off boyfriend, the one Humph met at the empty apartment, had decamped.

"I reached him by phone. Karena said it was OK. I told him why I'd disappeared all of a sudden. He said he was happy to hear I was all right but the whole thing spooked him. He said he had just left their apartment and moved in with a buddy to Jersey."

The apartment was in the young man's name, Eve said.

"I didn't really have much there to call my own. He said he took my clothes to his new place. He said I could pick them up anytime as if I'm going to go all the way across the river."

"Let's wait on that for a while," Humph said. He felt a vague relief that the young man had decided to part ways with Eve. He didn't seem to have much going for him. Eve would be better off in the end. Then his mind jumped to something even less promising than that relationship. The possibility of Eve getting together with Frankie.

Wheels screeching on tracks drowned his thoughts as they headed to Frankie's. Eve seemed glad to be out of the house.

She was impressed by the substantial homes on Frankie's tree-lined street.

Humph pointed out Frankie's place just ahead.

"It belongs to his father, like everything else in Frankie's life. But it's now Frankie's place."

"Never thought being filthy rich would be tough," Eve said.

As they climbed the few stone steps to the door, Frankie appeared with his right arm extended to usher them inside.

As Humph passed Frankie, the young man flashed a smile and said, "No booze. I know. I know."

Once inside the foyer, Humph let Frankie go ahead. He wanted to be in a position to see how Frankie greeted Eve.

A moment later, Willy, the little British butler arrived apologizing for his tardiness.

"Can you find some non-alcoholic refreshments for my guests?"

"Of course, sir. If I recall correctly, Mr. Humph was partial to lemonade. And for the young lady?" he said, turning to Eve, who was to Frankie's left.

"Lemonade, please." She sat on the sofa and Humph took his place beside her, facing Frankie in the grand antique easy chair.

Humph began:

"Frankie, you contacted Eve to get information for your story. I'm still annoyed that you didn't go through me. Be that as it may, I brought her here today for the purposes of your research. I might be able to fill in the details from an investigative perspective, but as I told you before, it's still premature to write about the whole ball of wax. If you blew a very large police investigation by publishing prematurely, I'd see to it that you'd never publish a word again in this town. I'm not only connected with the *New York World*. I include other influential publications among my contacts. Are we clear?"

"As a spring morning, Humph."

"Fine. Glad to hear it. Just remember, I have a witness to that promise."

"Of course, Humph. Don't worry."

"Go on. Hit Eve with your questions."

"All I know basically is that you were kidnapped. Where did it happen, at your place, at your work, on the street? And who did it?"

Eve had to say she had no idea at first why she'd been kidnapped or by whom.

"All I know now is what Humph has told me and he told me all that kind of stuff is just so much speculation at the moment."

"All we can say Frankie is that there seems to be a connection between the broker who bilked you out of ten Gs and a certain gangster who runs speakeasies and imports large quantities of Canadian whiskey. I'm telling you this only so you can start piecing together an outline or whatever you call it of what you going to write. But that's as far as it goes."

Frankie nodded. He spent the next half hour asking Eve for her feelings during the kidnapping and afterwards, and for the little personal details and fears that, as Frankie put it, can make a story sing.

As Frankie's questions petered out, he turned to Humph.

"This is great stuff."

"Good. You can hail your man Willy if you wish."

"Willy! Willy!" Frankie's voice resonated through half the house.

Poor Willy, thought Humph.

Without Frankie having given him instructions, Willy arrived with the drinks trolley and a bucket of ice.

As the drinks were being served, Eve and Frankie started to engage in small talk. After taking one sip of his lemonade, Humph put an end to that.

"There remains one stick of dynamite I need to explode right here in your salon, Frankie, in this very house that I know to be owned by your father in addition to all the fine furnishings."

"What in the hell are you talking about?" asked Frankie, whose slight smile showed he suspected a joke more than a bombshell of some kind.

Humph paused for another, heartier sip of his drink,

delaying long enough for the hint of a smile to disappear from Frankie's face.

With a gentleness that surprised himself, Humph quickly summarized the NYPD investigation in Montreal that involved a giant distillery and the trucking of their whiskey to New York in New York-registered vehicles.

"The NYPD's investigator, a man of long acquaintance, unearthed a fact that might turn your world upside down, Frankie. So let me just be out with it.

"In short, it is this: I was the one who first wondered whether your father, who you said has made a habit of visiting Montreal since you were just a lad, had any involvement with bootlegging Canadian whiskey. After all, he owns so many companies, I thought it was highly possible that one of them was a carrier."

"So?" said Frankie.

"My friend, the cop in Montreal, got hold of purchase orders for booze that we later learned was trucked to New York. Fine and dandy. We knew that might be a possibility. But, listen closely, Frankie. Here is the dynamite discovery I mentioned earlier. The purchase orders were made out not to your father, Mr. Randall Overton. Instead they were made out to Frankie Overton."

The drink dropped out of Frankie's hand. Humph and Eve watched as shock gave way to fury on Frankie's face. Frankie grabbed the lemonade pitcher that still sat on the coffee table and flung it across the room.

"Bastard! The fucking bastard! I'll kill him!"

Humph stood and approached the young man, placing a firm grip on his shoulders. Humph had the answer he needed. Frankie was not involved in the bootlegging.

When Frankie cooled down enough to talk, he asked over and over again:

"How could he? How could he? My own fucking father."

Humph then administered what could very well be the coup de grace.

"I can't prove it yet, but something tells me your father may have persuaded the stockbroker to set you up for a $10,000 fall. Why he would do that, I don't know. Why the broker would go along with that, I don't know. But we will do everything we can to find out. I promise you, Frankie. That's a kind of promise I don't usually make."

Frankie just stared right through Eve and Humph. He sat utterly motionless. At last, he said so softly Humph wasn't sure he heard right.

"I can't talk right now. Please…"

Humph stood and Eve followed. Willy appeared out of nowhere and led them to the door.

Eve didn't speak until they had gone through two jam-packed cars and found a seat on the homeward-bound train.

"I'd die if I heard something like that about you or Mom."

Humph hugged her, a quick, little hug. He was in a public place. People Eve's age didn't seem to mind public hugs and even kisses. Humph wasn't old, just 39, but this decade was demonstrating a willingness to make dinosaurs out of the common man's notions of decency.

He looked around the subway car. He wanted to say, "She's my daughter. It's OK if I hug her." Funny, he thought, how he'd fearlessly faced gangs of kids looking to pummel him half to death for no reason or to thrust a knife inches from his neck. He'd remain so courageously stoic in those circumstances his attackers sensed the wisdom of finding another mark. But public displays of affection? Maybe he was a dinosaur. End of story

CHAPTER 22

HUMPH tried phoning Frankie the next day to make sure he was alright. He tried in the morning and afternoon. Willy said, "I'm sorry, sir Humph. He has not descended from his room." On Humph's final attempt, Willy volunteered that his master had left the premises. "It is my understanding, sir, that the young gentleman has gone to a place called Atlantic City."

Humph thanked Willy. Was Atlantic City and its temptations the best place for Frankie? Perhaps. But maybe not. The glittering boardwalk world portrayed in the ads that reached all 48 states was run by Enoch Johnson. Just the other day in the paper there was a photo of him on the Boardwalk with none other than Meyer Lansky and Al Capone. What the hell was Frankie up to?

Frankie had a rich kid's connections but he didn't move in that league.

Humph ambushed Duffy at his place. He told him about the improbable connection of Frankie and America's most notorious and untouchable mobsters.

Duffy pondered and pondered. Was he hungover, wondered Humph, or seriously weighing the possibilities?

"No way, Humph. Neither the kid nor his old man has that kind of reach. It's just coincidence that Frankie is in Atlantic City when those guys are. Have you been there, Humph? At any given moment there are more famous Americans there at the same time than even New York. Nucky Jonson is the North Fucking Pole. Mobsters and politicians get zapped into his universe willing or not. He was the magnet at the heart of Eastern seaboard crime. I'm sure the president himself wishes he could think of some medal to give him."

Humph had little choice but to accept Duffy's nay. He decided to await his return. Why did it matter so much what he did or didn't do? Humph asked himself again and again and each time the answer was that he didn't want Eve anywhere near Frankie at the moment.

A week later, still with no word from Frankie, Humph opened the paper and saw a headline that might have either confirmed or killed his investigation, or more accurately, the NYPD's investigation:

"Big-Time Broker Bludgeoned". The headline ran right across the top of the paper.

The broker was none other than Reginald Ostenbruch.

Humph couldn't resist a sigh of relief. However, the details of the murder were curious. It wasn't a mugging. It didn't happen by chance. It happened in his own Gramercy Park residence. The killer had a purpose. He knew things.

The paper said nothing in the lavishly appointed dwelling had been stolen or even damaged. It was clear that the killer had one purpose: Kill Ostenbruch. Did the broker's advice cost the killer a fortune on the stock market?

"Frankie will love that story," thought Humph.

Again he tried to contact him by phone. The butler's response hadn't changed. He wasn't at home.

Humph decided he could write most of the story about the bootlegging and kidnapping now that he didn't have to wait for charges to be brought against the broker.

"We've got him," Duffy said. "Six ways to Sunday, he's going down."

As for Madden, Duffy told Humph that detectives had made inquiries at Madden's hotel of choice in Arkansas. They said the gangsters had departed along with a lot of what the hotel manager referred to as "Mr. Madden's employees." The manager said he assumed they went back to New York.

He spent three days manipulating a pencil over sheet after sheet of paper. The crossed-out lines outnumbered the acceptable ones. At the end of the three days of torture, the pencil was but a stub, so small Humph could barely pick it up.

"Maybe," Humph thought, "writing isn't for me."

Nevertheless, he took his desecrated journalistic masterpiece to the World to see what his contact Gerald Franklin thought of it.

Gerald started reading. He squinted a lot to make out the corrections. After almost five minutes, he said:

"Humph, I've been reading for longer than most people spend reading a newspaper article and I still don't know what the story is. A reader has to know in the first paragraph."

Humph had feared just that reaction but he said he didn't know how to do that.

"I can see that you've done a lot of work. That's a pile of pages," he said, pointing the Humph's story on his desk. "Maybe we should go with one of the ideas we came up with when we assigned you this story. I'll put your story in the hands of one of our crime reporters and after a day or two, when he's had a chance to find the essential story, he can take a crack at rewriting it. When he's done he'll call you and the two of you can arrange to go over it together to make sure he's got the story right. What say you?"

Instead of feeling deprived of the chance to see his very own words in print, Humph was relieved. He learned that he didn't know how to give order to a long story full of facts and twists and turns. However Gerald had made it clear that he had delivered on his promise to give the paper a doozy of a story. For now, all he had to worry about would be massaging away the cramp in his writing hand.

As well as not having heard back from Frankie, he hadn't talked to Eve in days. He decided to knock on Karena's door that evening. A phone call told him she was working day shift of late. Eve would probably be home as well.

Humph had had enough of sitting around at his kitchen table. The day was beautiful and not too hot. A walk would do him good, he decided. He first went to the Bowery, thinking of dropping in on Duffy on the off chance he'd be home. As he neared it, he changed his mind. God knows what Duffy might rope him into.

Instead he turned east to Rivington Street. He made a beeline to the bath house. It had been a week since he'd enjoyed a hot shower. The Rivington Street Bath House was large. They offered 91 showers and 10 baths. But as soon as he stepped inside, he knew he'd be lucky to find a stall. The place was jammed. However he had to wait only 10 minutes. The hot water did wonders. Even his cramped hand had recovered enough to do up shirt buttons without wincing.

As he stepped out onto the street, he no longer debating the advisability of dropping in on Karena that evening. He told himself he was dropping in on Officer Melchinskaya, a colleague of sorts. Under the blanket of official business, he was also visiting Karena, the striking blond Ukrainian woman who he suspected knew how to show Eve the kind of affection she hadn't known since her mother died. She must be a great comfort to Eve.

At the same time, Humph realized it wasn't just that quality that drew him to her. On their very first meeting in the captain's office he was attracted to her physically. In fact, he realized that the very instant she stood and shook his hand. She looked Humph straight in the eye. It wasn't a quick, nervous look. There was nothing perfunctory nor shy about it. She actually looked at him. At least that's what Humph told himself when he got home.

Because a huge part of him believed he'd never find another Sunny, and a good portion of the rest of him said walking into another relationship would somehow be sacrilege, he rarely noticed women other than as sources of investigative information. Although he wouldn't admit it at the time, Edith had begun to penetrate his defenses. Her murder was shocking by any standard but Humph felt actual loss, personal loss, when he learned she'd been killed. Even the act of going through the documents her lifeless body collapsed on made him sad despite the fact they provided good information linking her boss to trucking, illegal booze and the gangster. He understood the pain that devoured friends and loved ones of crime victims but he was too professional to reflect on tragedy for more than a few seconds. Perhaps he instinctively felt no one else's pain could equal his.

Even Eve, Sunny's daughter, had more than once urged Humph to move on. She even said her mom would have wanted that.

When Humph knocked on Officer Melchinskaya's door two hours later, he strongly needed a focus to escape the three-ring circus in his head.

"Humph! How are you?" Karena met him with a big smile. "Come in. Come in." She led Humph to a big chair and immediately asked if he'd heard from Eve lately.

Humph was taken aback. He assumed that Eve would either be there or that at least Karena would know of her whereabouts.

It had been several days since he'd heard from Eve or had news of her. He had been working hard to not expect her to call daily. Before this whole mess, he usually saw her only on her monthly visits. She was a grown woman with her own life.

Karena said the last news she had from Eve was her happy announcement that she and Frankie were going to Atlantic City for a few days.

"It didn't shock me enough to call you, Humph. In fact, I thought it would be good for her to get out of here for starters and secondly that she'd be safer out of town that in New York."

Humph couldn't fault her reasoning. His immediate concern was that he didn't know Frankie well enough to know whether he'd behave.

"When Eve told me about Frankie's invitation to join her, she was as excited as a schoolgirl. I remember her words. 'It's what the doctor ordered, Karena. A first-class hotel, first-class food, a bit of gambling with someone else's money, and a sweet, handsome guy to lead the way.' Humph, I would have happily exchanged places with her.

"She said that she and Frankie had talked many times about the details of the kidnapping, the speakeasy-bordello-dancehall place and the slimy broker who got bumped."

Humph was relieved to learn that Frankie was serious about writing his detective-magazine article. He wouldn't do anything to spoil his relationship with a dream informant, the victim herself.

Karena placed a whiskey in Humph's hand. She then sat on the sofa.

"Join me here, Humph."

Though he was supremely comfortable in the easy chair after days spent on the wooden chair at his place, he obeyed.

Karena was still wearing her uniform pants. She hadn't been expecting a visit from Humph. She explained that she had spent the afternoon part of her shift doing exactly what Humph used to do, and what led to him meeting Sunny. She was on prostitute patrol. More specifically, she was assigned to chat up the street girls and any suspicious activity they, or their johns, might be up to. The girls talked more openly with a female cop, especially a young pretty one. More than one said Karena should dump the uniform and join them.

"You'd make a killing, girl," one said.

Humph was on the verge of describing how he met Eve's mom, then stopped himself. Too early to share that, he decided.

While they chatted generally about the case, Humph was interrogating himself. "Was it too early to share something like that? Am I still hiding?" Sunny used to tease him about not sharing his feelings. She called him a coward, like almost every man she'd ever known. She didn't live long enough to find out that Humph wanted desperately to share every bit of himself with her.

Not long after arriving, Humph offered to take Karena out to eat.

"I'm sure if we walk up to Grand Street we'll find something good."

Karena raised her hand.

"No, Humph. I've got to stay by the phone in case Eve calls. I'm technically on duty, not that I'm being paid for the time." She laughed. Humph smiled back. He put his right hand on her left shoulder. "I thank you for your sacrifice, Karena." He liked saying her name, even the multi-syllable last name. Mel-chin-ska-ya. To his ears, there was something courageous and fiery about it.

When he told Karena that she exclaimed that "All Ukrainian people are courageous. They have to be because of the damned Bolsheviks. They defeated us a few years ago and we've hated them and Stalin ever since. I was one of the lucky ones to escape."

Humph pulled her to him, staring into her eyes, still passionate from the expression of defiance and hate. She didn't resist. They kissed. As they broke apart, Karena held Humph's hand.

"To the kitchen. We will cook together!"

Humph stayed the night, thankful for a million things in life, including the time spent at the Rivington Bath House.

The phone rang early the next morning. The first call was from Karena's captain, telling her she'd be working the evening shift. There was another suspected speakeasy to bust.

The second call was from none other than Duffy.

"Sir," he said by way of hello.

"Fuck you, Duffy." She was smiling at Humph as she said it.

"She swears at work and wears pants at home. I like that," Humph thought.

As Karena related a few minutes later, Duffy had called to say that they'd arrested the man who killed Edith. After an 18-hour interrogation without a restroom break for the suspect, he admitted to doing the deed on orders from a Mr. Reginald Ostenbruch, or at least one of his henchmen. The suspect proclaimed the little woman he stabbed to death was suspected of stealing confidential company information. Karena said Duffy expressed great enjoyment at the fact that the suspect released "a Niagara of urine" in his pants at one point. He said that the smell "didn't bother him in the slightest."

"Case closed," exclaimed Humph, pulling Karena into his arms again.

CHAPTER 23

"HI, Humph. I'm back. I know Karena told you where I've been."

"And…?" replied Humph.

"I felt like a queen. No kidding. Limousines whenever we went anywhere. Can you believe that?"

"What is a limousine exactly?"

"I guess it's just a gorgeous car driven by a man with a little hat. Here's what we always drove in. I wrote it down. It was a Rolls Royce Phantom Limousine. It was white like the caps of the waves you see there on the beach on a windy day. I can't believe I live in New York and have never seen the ocean, Humph. You gotta go to Coney Island or those other beaches. I'd be happy to go with you."

Then Eve added:

"You could also go with Karena. I know she'd love that."

"Eve! How do you know that, that she'd like to join us?"

Eve's laughter refused to stop. Finally, Karena came on the line.

"Girls talk, Humph. So when are you renting a Rolls Royce limousine and taking Eve and I to the beach?"

Humph knew when he was beaten. He wondered what else they'd talked about. Did Eve know he and Karena were, were, were... He never finished the thought. Someone was at his door. Humph quickly said goodbye to Eve.

"Karena says 'bye' too."

It had better be a man at the door, Humph thought.

As Humph went to open the door he was thinking that the conspiring women in his life had set this up. A double whammy. First, Eve knows about Karena. Second, they've set up a meeting with Eve's new lover.

Frankie was not exactly the man Humph was hoping to see.

Humph shook his hand. While returning the gesture, Frankie assessed the apartment.

"Almost quaint, Humph."

Thank goodness that the kid smiled as he said it, thought Humph. He was teasing, Humph decided for Eve's sake. The kid wouldn't be leaving with a mashed mouth.

Frankie turned down the offer of a drink.

"I have to stay sharp, Humph. Believe it or not, I am actually writing my story about all these criminal wheelings and dealings, and murders. What a case!"

"Were you writing in Atlantic City?"

"As a matter of fact, I was. Eve has been a huge help."

"How so?"

"Well, first, the first-hand evidence and descriptions. The magazine loves that. And secondly, she really knows the seamy side of life in New York. I've read about it, of course, Humph. But your Eve has experienced it. She's saved my story from a million false assumptions already, and I haven't finished."

"What about the rest of the time, when the two of you weren't writing?"

Frankie laughed.

"Everything was *comme il faut.*"

"What the hell does that mean? Should I hit you or congratulate you?"

"It means everything was on the up and up, proper as can be. Relax. I'm here about my story."

"Forgive me. I've had one too many surprises in recent days. And by that I mean you hauling Eve to Atlantic City without notifying me."

Humph couldn't hide his anger.

"Humph, I tried to call you. There was no answer. I even asked Eve whether you'd object and she said you treated her like a grown woman. What else was I supposed to do?"

Humph didn't have an answer.

"You may not want one but I'm going to pour myself a drink," Humph said.

When he returned, he chose to sit rather than on one of the chairs he'd grown to hate.

"Sorry, Frankie. It's just that Eve's like a daughter. But she told you straight. She's her own woman. I don't control her."

Frankie exhaled deeply.

"Glad that's settled. I always suspected that you can be as soft-spoken as you want but there's a hell of a temper wrapped up inside of you."

Humph didn't deny it.

"How can I help you? I mean your story," he said.

Humph filled him in on the case against the broker, at least the one the DA had been hoping to pursue before Ostenbruch was murdered.

"Can't say I cried for him," said Frankie.

"Me neither but for different reasons," said Humph.

"He had a friend of mine killed. A secretary who worked for him. A sweet and honest young woman who just wanted to see justice done. Look in the newspaper archives or the library. Her name was Edith. The information she'd given me kicked off the NYPD investigation into him, Owney Madden and, I'm sorry to say, your father.

"This is the part you still can't write about. I've already told you that he has involved you in all this by using your name instead of his on purchase orders for booze. But you've got to promise not to publish before this information is confirmed by NYPD. And you have to promise not to kill the bastard for what he did to you."

"I promise. I promise, Humph. But please give me what you know now so I can add it to my story and be ready to publish the instant you give the go-ahead."

"If you screw me over, Frankie, you will have lost your relationship with Eve and you will have gained the enemy of your nightmares."

The expression on Frankie's face suggested he believed Humph.

"I'm getting another drink," said Humph. The real reason he said that was to give himself time to evaluate the kid's reaction to being told not to act on what he'd been told about his father. There was no reaction. Frankie acted like it was just another little fact to add to his story when the time came. He didn't reveal what Humph would have considered a normal reaction. Surely, he would want to make his father pay big time.

Frankie sensed that Humph was suspicious.

"Look Humph. The idea that my father wanted to screw me over came as no surprise. I hate the man and have since I was a kid. I am happy as hell that I now know that when I publish my story all the world to see what a bastard his is."

Humph decided he had to take the kid's word.

They spent the next hour going over the small details of the case.

The downside for Humph was that without nailing Madden on something, they couldn't shut down the speaks acting as de facto brothels. Humph didn't care about speaks. Americans should be free to drink. But the question of brothels had become a personal fight.

Frankie realized for the first time how personal this was for the big man.

"Humph, I hear you. Really. I want my story to tell about the biggest takedowns in New York history. I want it to be such a sensation that my writing will be in demand for a very long time."

Maybe Frankie was legit.

By the end of August, Frankie had stopped calling. He said he'd basically written the entire story and was just waiting on a green light from Humph about his father's situation. Humph knew where the case stood. As far as he, a former cop, was concerned, they had Frankie's old man dead to rights. But he also had learned that justice had a different sense of time when the rich were involved.

Eve, on the other hand, visited Humph often. She was clearly in love with the young writer with thick, wavy dark hair and a handsome disregard for public opinion. They went to Manhattan clubs where even a stripper found her eyes glued wide open. She also delighted in the restaurants and the gowns only people like Frankie could afford. He was a good lover, she decided, and stingy wasn't in his vocabulary. Her only regret, she told Humph, was that they hadn't found a white Rolls-Royce for hire in New York.

In mid-September, Duffy invited Humph out for drinks at the bar next to the precinct. He said it was the one and only place for revealing NYPD triumphs. He refused to say more over the phone.

When Humph arrived, there was a barstool with a piece of paper stuck to it. "Barstal's stool!"

Several cops ordered him to sit at the same time.

Duffy installed himself next Humph.

"I wanted you to be the first outsider to know that we've nailed dear Pillar of Society, Mr. Randall Overton. A smuggler he is, Humph. He's being arraigned at this very moment. We've got everyone except Madden but we don't need him. We'll get his Irish ass another day."

Humph's eyes lit up.

"Now that's a rare sight, Humph. You're always so damned detached about things."

Humph excused himself and went outside to a public phone. His first call was to Frankie. To his surprise, Frankie barely reacted to the news.

"Humph, nothing about my dad surprises me. In fact, I don't feel a thing."

"The point is," interrupted Humph, "is that you're now free to finish your article and publish."

"By God, you're right. I was so wrapped up in my hatred for my old man I forgot the most important way I can defy him. Be a writer."

"Let me know when the article comes out, Frankie. I'll be first in line, or rather second. Right after Eve."

Humph ran back into the bar to ask a cop for a nickel to make another phone call.

"Give, give, give," insisted Humph. "The next beer's on me," he said, thrusting a dollar bill in the cop's hand.

The call he made was to the *New York World*.

"Sorry, sir, Mr. Franklin has gone home for the night."

"Give me his number."

"We can't do that, sir."

Suddenly, the name of the reporter who been assigned to rewrite his story came to mind.

"Is Walter Tomkins there?"

"Yes, sir. I'll put you through."

"Slow down, slow down," Tomkins said as Humph relayed the news that the final piece of the puzzle had been solved.

Humph opened the phone booth door and inhaled deeply.

"OK, Walter. I'm all yours. Tell me what you need."

Walter told him he had basically finished assembling the story. Adding the arraignment of the big shot society guy was easy.

"It'll all be in tomorrow's paper, Humph. Great work."

Humph walked home. He felt he was in a dream. He was in bed before he remembered that he'd left Duffy waiting for him.

He went to sleep dreaming of Karena.

CHAPTER 24

THE phone woke Humph the next morning. He was now regretting having become modern.

"It's Duffy. Where the fuck did you disappear to last night?"

Humph couldn't immediately remember deserting him. Finally, he remembered calling Frankie and the newspaper.

"Sorry, Duffy. I had some important calls to make. I just forgot after."

Duffy answered that he might as well have remained the drunk he used to be if he was going to mess up like that.

Humph laughed.

"Never, Duffy. By the way, what time does the *New York World* hit the streets?"

"It already has."

"Get a copy, right now. Check out the byline of the lead story. Call me back when you've read it, my friend."

Humph put on the coffee. He was in a daze. Things had happened so fast. '

Half an hour later, the phone rang.

"Humph, your story isn't at the top of the page."

"What the hell are you talking about?"

"There's a showbiz story there. The headline reads, 'Silent Movie Era Over'. A movie with sound hit the theaters last night. It's called *The Jazz Singer*. It stars Al Jolson. At the bottom of the story they say, 'See Murder, Kidnapping, Bootlegging by Humphrey Barstal, Page 4-5."

"Call me back in 10 minutes, Duff."

Humph dashed out to the corner kiosk and bought a copy of the paper. Standing at the busy intersection in his pajamas, he thumbed his way to the spread on Page 4-5.

It was all there. The whole story. The whole case. And his name was even in bold-face type.

"Sir," said the man behind the pile of papers and magazines, "that will be two cents."

Without thinking, Humph reached for the change, only to realize he was still wearing pajamas.

"I'll be right back with your two cents."

Just after he got back home, the phone rang. It was Frankie, not Duffy.

"Congratulations, Humph. You've been published and I hope to be soon. I'm truly grateful, big guy. I'm mailed you a final payment. I think you'll like the amount."

Abruptly, Frankie hung up. A moment later, Duffy called back.

"We have to celebrate, Humph. But you gotta promise not to walk out on me again, like a bride at the altar."

"I promise," said Humph.

The morning was starting far too fast. He lay down and stared at the ceiling. All he heard was silence, something that never happened in Chinatown.

Humph dozed off. He woke up curled like a baby. He reached out with one hand without opening his eyes. Nothing. He lowered the hand. The floor. He forced a breath, exhaling then inhaling. His eyes opened. Thank god it was still daylight. It had been the sleep of the dead.

Getting up, he walked straight to the intruder in his home, the phone.

He dialed. Eve answered.

"Humph. I just heard. The paper says Frankie's dad is dead."

He hadn't heard. He wondered whether anyone involved in this case was going to keep breathing long enough to make a court appearance.

"Sorry, Eve. I just woke up. I'm just trying to digest your news. By the way, why do you sound so happy?"

"Well…"

The pause was long.

"Well, Frankie's happy, too. In fact, he's crazy happy. He said he, and me, we are about to inherit an absolute fortune. Frankie was the only kid and the old man's wife is long dead. We're going to inherit everything, Humph. I'm going to be rich. And if I'm rich, believe me, please believe me, you're going to be rich. If only Mom was alive to be rich, too."

It was all too good to be true, thought Humph. He felt depressed all of a sudden.

"Eve, dear. Please wait. These things, inheritances, all that can be complicated. We have no idea what Frankie's dad stipulated. Don't celebrate yet, and above all don't spend the money you think you're getting. Stick to creamed chipped beef on toast."

"You're no fun, Humph. No fun at all."

"Love you," Humph said, hanging up before Eve could respond.

Full of questions he couldn't justify, Humph kept to himself for the next two days. When he surfaced from his reflections, he called the only person he thought could help. Karena.

"Hi, Humph. I thought you were ignoring me."

"Never," Humph said, surprised that he came up with a good answer rather than mumbling excuses that she would never been believed. Karena was someone who seemed able to digest nothing but the truth. How do you get like that? Humph sure as hell didn't know but he knew it was an admirable trait.

"I read a lot, Karena, but Shakespeare said something I don't know much about. Something about something stinking in Denmark. I guess you didn't study Shakespeare in Ukraine."

"No, but I went to high school right here on the Lower East Side. Lots of Shakespeare and Dickens. And as for the stench in Denmark, the line was something being rotten in the state of Denmark. Hamlet."

"You're right, Karena. That's exactly what I feel about Frankie's expectation of inheriting his father's millions. And I don't expect I need to add that Eve is hoping to become rich at the same time."

"Have you read the latest editions of the paper?"

"No."

"Well, it says he was killed in Montreal, not New York. In fact, the murder took place at the Ritz Hotel."

"His rich acquaintances will undoubtedly approve of where Overton shuffled off this mortal coil," interrupted Humph.

"I see you do read Shakespeare," Karena said. "And I see that you are far more cynical that I could have imagined."

Karena continued.

"It says he was shot at almost point-blank range in the back. The bullet lodged in his heart. But the police don't know or won't say yet who did it. There's no one in custody."

Karena said Overton had just finished dining and had gone to the cloakroom by the entrance to the restaurant to retrieve his raincoat. Apparently, the weather forecast called for thunderstorms and showers for the rest of the day.

"The story goes on to say the hat check girl was hysterical for many minutes after the shooting.

She denied any involvement and the police don't consider her a suspect."

"Do the cops have any suspects?" Humph asked.

"None that are mentioned," Karena replied. "All they said was that a good number of people were passing between the cloakroom, located on one side of a relatively narrow entrance, and the maître d's lectern, or whatever you call it, on the other side. The maître d' says his back was to the restaurant as he greeted new arrivals. And the poor girl in the cloak room says she only saw the gentleman crumble forwards and fall to the floor. It was all a blur, she said."

What a peculiar incident, thought Humph. Why choose a busy hotel to take someone down? Why not shoot him when he was out of sight, in his room, or the restroom perhaps?"

"Well," said Karena. "It's not our case."

"We'll see," said Humph. "I'll call you later."

"I'm working tonight," Karena said. "Call tomorrow afternoon if you want to."

That evening, Humph used his new best friend to call Duffy at the precinct.

"What's your take on Overton's murder in Montreal? Is it true they have no suspects?"

"Right you are," said Duffy. "At the precinct I asked them to send me back to Montreal to talk to their cops but no one would hear of it."

"Or," suggested Humph, "they simply thought you wanted to explore more of those lovely bistro places you raved about on your last trip."

"Not everyone has the gift of seeing the bigger picture like we do, Humph. Anyway, all I can do right now is phone a detective I met there and open some avenues of inquiry for him."

"Such as?"

"Such as the fact Overton had a Montreal mistress. Or the fact that he was a majority shareholder in the city's largest distillery. Or that we have tied him to a New York broker who recently had the bad luck of being bludgeoned to death and the fact that it was likely he had business dealings with one of Ireland's finest gangsters, operating in New York these many years."

Humph congratulated Duffy on the case he had put together to present to his brothers in blue in Montreal.

"I'll keep you posted," said Duffy, hanging up.

That night, Humph had already gone to bed when the phone rang. It was Duffy again.

"Pull your britches on, Humph. We've got some drinking to do. Meet me in the usual place."

Before Humph fully registered what Duffy had said, the line went dead.

While getting dressed, he swore mightily at the Irishman. While combing his hair, the force in his fingers broke the comb.

As he entered the bar half an hour later, Duffy's voice rose above the usual din of half-inebriation. He was singing an unrecognizable tune but nobody minded. It was party time for some reason.

As Humph edged his way next to his friend, Duffy suddenly stopped signing and punched Humph's shoulder so hard he hurt his fist.

"What the hell, Duffy!"

"Hear this, Humph," he said, grabbing Humph's lapel. Then, more loudly, he echoed his own words. "Now hear this one an all!"

"Hear what?" several cops replied, playing the game.

"Charles Duffy will henceforth be known to the world as Detective Sergeant Charles Duffy of the New York Police Department!"

Duffy had already removed his jacket so Humph grabbed him by the scruff of the neck and pulled his face close to his.

With his eyes just inches below Humph's and peering up, Duffy exclaimed:

"Yes, fucking yes, fucking yes! You heard right, Humph. After I talked to you this afternoon, the lieutenant called me in and said I'd been promoted."

"To my surprise, my total surprise, they said my work in the bootlegging and murder case set me apart from the run of the mill officer in this department. And they said my work in Montreal was detective-grade policing."

For the first time in the years they'd known each other, Humph saw tears in his friend's eyes.

"They should hire you back, Humph, as a detective. It was your investigation that made this possible."

Humph smiled and shook his hand warmly. Several of his foot patrol buddies began a chant of "Three cheers for Duffy, three cheers for the Irish."

When they quieted down, Humph pulled Duffy to a table where he asked, "What's your first assignment going to be, detective?"

"Whatever it is, Humph, I'm going to refuse it."

"On your first day?" said Humph.

"Damn right, Humph. I'm going to tell them I have an investigation to finish in Montreal. They won't be able to say no this time."

Humph stayed for an hour then slipped out the door and headed home. He doubted that Duffy would be capable of reporting for duty for his first shift as a detective. As for himself, Humph hadn't forgotten he might be able to see Karena the next day. The feeling had crept up on him slowly and silently but he now knew with absolute certainty that he wanted this woman in his life.

CHAPTER 25

WHEN Humph got to Karena's place, he found both Karena and Eve there. At the door, Karena held Humph's hand for the briefest moment before showing him to a chair next to hers. Eve leapt up from the sofa and gave him a hug.

Eve and Karena started to talk at the same time. Karena let Eve speak first.

"Frankie asked me to tell you that he has started writing his article for *True Manhattan Detective* magazine. He says he's making great progress thanks to you. He said the story will be better than any of the radio scripts he wrote for CBS."

"I hope," replied Humph, "that he remembers that what he wrote for radio was fiction. Our story is not."

Karena asked Eve whether she and Frankie were already living the good life that his inheritance would all but guarantee.

Eve laughed.

"As far as I'm concerned, Karena, everything about Frankie's old life was life high on the hog. He doesn't talk much about the inheritance. He wants to focus on his story. More than anything in life he wants to see his byline in a magazine. The only mention he has ever made about it was the fact that his lawyer told him he won't reveal anything about the will until Mr. Overton's body has been returned to New York for burial.

"It should be back already," Karena said. "Montreal police told us the body had been released three days after the murder. It would arrive in New York the same day. Frankie must have been notified, surely."

Eve looked puzzled, too.

"I guess he has a lot on his mind right now," Eve said with a shrug. "I must say it's a bit strange, though, that he doesn't seem to mourn his dad's passing even a little bit."

"Don't blame him," said Humph. "I can't imagine being treated like that by a father. He wanted to destroy his son. Why? I have no idea. A powerful rich man who's crazy to boot is a dangerous thing. It's a wonder Frankie stayed sane."

As Humph mouthed those words, he realized he still harbored suspicions about Frankie. His transformation from rich party boy to professional writer was somehow all too easy. But as often as he'd reviewed every conversation the two had had, he couldn't put his finger on anything. In the end, all Humph hoped for was that Frankie would write a true account of the big investigation.

Humph then said, "Let's forget about Frankie for now. How are you doing, Eve?"

"I was wondering that, too," said Karena. "You haven't been here a lot."

222

Eve started to give the answer that had become pat since she started having an affair with Frankie, namely that she was "Great!" Then she realized she was in the presence of two professional investigators.

"To be perfectly frank, no pun intended, being a rich guy's girlfriend can be boring, boring, boring. I know he's too busy for me right now with all that's happened but when I think about how it might be when it's all over I still can see more boredom than I want. I miss being a stripper. I miss being a dancer learning a part for a burlesque act. I never had money to go to nice restaurants or clubs on my own and I honestly never spent much time imagining doing those things. If a rich son of a bitch like Ostenbruch wanted to pretend he was on a date with a pretty young stripper, I'd be happy to let him pay. I just made sure to stay sober enough to fight off his hands."

Humph was pleased with the answer, although he said nothing. Eve was still hard-working, street-smart Eve.

Eve then said, "Enough about me. Why don't you guys go out and paint the town red!"

Humph was about to say something about hating the smell of paint but fortunately for him Karena got her words out first.

"Wonderful idea, Eve. Come, help me decide what to wear." With that, the two of them disappeared into the bedroom. It was almost half an hour before they emerged. Gone was Karena's uniform. In its place, a simple coral dress that was not designed to camouflage curves. Eve had obviously worked on her hair as well.

"Well, Humph?" said Eve, prodding him for a gallant reaction.

Humph was truly mesmerized. It was so obvious that no one expected a verbal reply from him.

Eve was grinning from ear to ear.

"Don't be late, you two," she said, closing the door behind them.

Humph had received Frankie's final payment. It was more than generous. Had Frankie mentioned the amount when they discussed payment, Humph would have said no to such an amount. Now he was happy to have it in a cookie jar labelled "Molasses".

On the street, he announced to Karena that they were going to the Cotton Club. It wasn't cheap but Humph was so attracted to Karena that he wanted to waste no time in proving it. She knew as well as he that a club that attracts countless celebrities wasn't meant for the budget of working stiffs.

When she started to object to the extravagance, Humph already has his reply memorized.

"Forgive me for sort of having an ulterior motive, Karena. First and foremost, I think I like jazz. Second, I keep reading about this place in the paper. As a detective, I'm curious by nature. And as for my ulterior motive, you may not know this but the place is owned by none other than Mr. Owney Madden, the very gentleman who has eluded us in our bootlegging investigation."

Karena laughed out loud.

"Let's do it, Humph. By the way, do you dance?"

The question punctured Humph's balloon. Karena had to grab his hand to get him moving toward a street where they might find a taxi.

When they arrived at 142ⁿᵈ Street and Lenox Avenue, the crowd on the sidewalk was close to what a cop would say was a potential mob scene. However, most people quickly made room for the white couple making their way to the club entrance. The line moved slowly. When Humph and Karena got to the head of the line, the bouncer shook his head, "No". Humph was about to move in close and tower over him, despite the man's burliness, but Karena flashed a smile and showed her badge.

"Police business," she said. The sea parted.

Their table wasn't the best but the atmosphere was

electric. On stage was the Duke himself. Ellington's orchestra had been the talk of New York for the past four years and for the city's high society, a visit to the Cotton Club to see Ellington was fast becoming de rigueur.

Neither Humph nor Karena recognized any of them for certain but many a face looked somewhat like faces they'd seen in newspapers. Several times when the music became unbearably possessive, Karena looked at Humph, hoping. Finally, she realized he wasn't about to risk embarrassment on the dance floor. Even without dancing, she was happy to be there. She'd never seen this side of the city.

She noticed as the evening wore on that Humph actually spent more than a few moments scanning the place, undoubtedly in the hopes of seeing Madden.

Around midnight, Karena confessed to being hungry. The truth was that she simply wanted to leave the club. Coming from Ukraine, she couldn't begin to ignore the fact that all those beautiful, talented performers were not the same color as the filthy rich patrons. She didn't want to be part of it anymore.

On the way home, she and Humph talked about racism. Humph was more used to it than she was.

"Karena, I've grown up here and the city is built on hatred and suspicion of anyone not born here with the color white and speaking English without an accent." It was a depressing thought even for him. "But it will change some day," he said, taking Karena's hand. "It has to."

Humph's spirits picked up. He felt blessed at having an outsider's view of America. Later, he told Karena that "you get so lost in the way things are that you simply stop believing in what things could be."

When Karena unlocked the door to her flat, Eve greeted them.

"Hi, kids!"

On his way home, Humph realized that was exactly how he felt after an evening with Karena.

CHAPTER 26

THE next morning Eve phoned Humph.

"Are you going to spy on me for the rest of my days, Eve?"

"Only when there's a girl involved."

They laughed the way they used to when she'd pay her monthly visit to his place.

"What's on your mind?" Humph asked.

"I don't know whether it's anything but I forgot to tell you before that Frankie went to Montreal once after I met him. I found it strange that he didn't say much about it afterwards. Just that he had childhood memories in the city and thought that now that he was a writer he might use them some day. I only thought of it today when I saw the stubs of some train tickets with the name Montreal Limited on the floor near his desk.

"It kind of made sense at the time. But I found it a bit strange that he didn't invite me. After all, he'd already taken me to Atlantic City and we had a great time together. I'd love to see Montreal."

Humph found the Montreal trip strange in a different way. Frankie's memories of the city were not pleasant in the slightest. That's where, as a boy, he began to realize he didn't mean much to his father. And for him to exclude Eve was indeed odd.

He didn't know what to make of it either but he told Eve he was grateful for the information, adding that the investigation of his father's murder was still open in Montreal.

"One more thing, Humph. The funeral for Frankie's father is tomorrow. I'll be going with him. The will is going be read the next day at his lawyer's office. Frankie's excited about that. I find that a bit strange as well, Humph. He already has a lot of money."

"Maybe he just wants to spend it on you, Eve."

Eve laughed.

"Love you," she said as she hung up.

Since Frankie had paid him in full, Humph no longer had an active case of his own. He didn't like leisure. Needing to stretch his legs, he walked up to the precinct station. His intent was merely to stick his nose in and see what might be going on. The first thing he noticed was that the holding cells were empty.

He caught the desk sergeant's eye and pointed toward them.

The sarge laughed.

"Your buddy Duffy wandered in here the night of his promotion. He was gloriously pissed. One minute he was making a speech about God knows what, then railing full voice against the punks who keep us busy. As he did so he pressed his face against the cell doors. I think the three guys we were holding pissed themselves. They were arraigned in the morning and we haven't welcomed a visitor since."

"I gather Duff didn't report in the next day."

"No and we're all glad he didn't. When he's hung over and bitching you just want to hit him."

The sergeant said Duffy showed up today, though. He's probably still suffering from his celebration but I think he's also happy as a pig in shite."

"Where can I find him?"

"I don't rightly know. Ask upstairs. One of the detectives will know."

Humph took the stairs two at a time just for the exercise.

"Anyone know where Duffy is?" he said, addressing the whole room.

A voice at the back said Duffy had gone to school.

"Yeah," said another detective, sitting at a desk beside Humph. "He needs to learn to keep his hands off the female merchandise he brings in. He's giving us all a bad name." The remark drew a moment's laughter. "No, seriously, we have some procedures a new detective wouldn't know about during his days in blue. Personally, I'm glad to have Duffy on board. He drinks hard but he works that way, too."

All the while he was talking, the detective's eyes were on the paperwork in front of him. When he finally looked up, his eyes lit up.

"Hey, Humph! Good to see you even though you deserted the department."

"Just wanted to be my own kind of detective, one with no lieutenants or captains or, God, deputy chiefs to answer to."

The two men shook hands.

"What do you want Duffy for?"

"A case he and I worked on for a long time. One of our suspects is being buried tomorrow. Thought Duffy might want to be there."

"Sure. Tell me when and where and I'll leave him a note."

As Humph left the station, he wondered whether Karena would be attending as well. Like Duffy, she didn't like the fact that the Montreal cops hadn't found a suspect yet for the murder of Frankie's dad.

That night, Karena told him she'd be there.

"Would you mind if I went with you?" Humph asked.

"God no, Humph. This is really all your case. If you still worked for NYPD you'd be up for promotion. Stop being so humble, Humph. I mean it."

The next morning was sunny but unusually chilly for September. When Karena arrived, Humph was standing in front of the Fifth Avenue Presbyterian Church. If no one had told him where the service would be held, Humph would have guessed it would be this church. The place was a landmark. It sat 2,000. Former president Teddy Roosevelt's mother and his first wife were both buried there. Humph was sure Overton always felt he belonged in company like that.

Karena and Humph sat near the back. They realized they could see very little. It was too late but they should have sat in the balcony looking down on the service. Nevertheless, it was the actual burial that interested them. Who would be shedding tears, whose face would betray a smirk? As they chatted in whispers, Humph felt someone jab him in the back. He turned and Karena followed. It was Duffy. He was standing just behind them.

When the service ended, the three of them stayed put and focused on the faces of the hundreds who had come to pay their respects "to the best New York society had to offer". Just before the church emptied, Humph spotted Frankie and Eve and waved them over to join them.

Suddenly Duffy erupted:

"You won't believe who just walked by. The dead guy's mistress from Montreal."

Before Humph could say a word, Duffy was gone. He sprinted out of the church ignoring the pastor's proffered handshake at the top of the steps. Seeing how crowded the sidewalk was, he stopped on the stairs and used the elevation to see better. No luck. There were hundreds of people on the sidewalk in front of the church. Frankie caught up with Duffy a moment later. "Do you see her?"

"No. She's gone, kid."

"Do you even know what she looks like?" Frankie asked Duffy.

"Yeah, the Montreal police had a photo of her. Someone from the Ritz told them your father had been dining with her. The restaurant staff said they often ate here together. They told the cops the camera girl in the lobby once took a photo of the two of them together. It was some time ago but the cops talked to the camera girl and she said she had a negative.

"Why would the cops want a photo of her?" asked Frankie.

"Just in case she saw anything just before the shooting. I don't know whether they ever located her."

To Duffy's eyes, there was something strange in the fact that Frankie appeared pleased by his answer.

They returned to the church and rejoined Humph, Eve and Karena. This time on his way out, Duffy shook the pastor's hand.

"I bet she's on the way to catch a train back to Montreal," said Humph.

"Maybe I could find her at Grand Central," said Duffy.

"A waste of time," said Humph. "She's not charged with anything. We have no business interrogating her."

"This is not over, Humph," mumbled Duffy. "I've got to go."

At 11 the next morning, Frankie and Eve arrived at his lawyer's office. They weren't alone. There was a dark-haired woman, 40-ish, attractive, already seated before the lawyer's desk. Frankie and Eve settled into the other two chairs.

"We all know why we're here," said the lawyer. The lawyer wasn't a big man but his desk was immense, the kind of furniture a firm can buy when their clients include the filthy rich. He had to stand in order to lean forward far enough to pass documents to each of the three people in front of him.

"Mr. Overton's last will and testament is extremely long because it entails instructions for dealing with his many properties and companies. You all are entitled to access this entire document but I suggest that we deal with the bestowals to family and friends. The three of you are the only ones mentioned in the will."

Frankie was dying to find out who the woman on his right was.

She said to the lawyer:

"Can we proceed, sir?"

Frankie now knew. Her accent was French. She was his dad's mistress from Montreal.

"Of course, madam," said the lawyer. "To the nitty gritty we go." He said it with a little smile.

"To my son Franklin, I leave the sum of $12 million dollars in cash, stocks and bonds in addition to my corporation's assets. In order to receive this inheritance, Franklin must sign a document to the effect that he engages to finally study the financial markets and become adept at buying and selling. His signature must be witnessed by a lawyer or notary. In addition, Frankie must present said attorney with proof of enrolment at a university that teaches the aforesaid skills. Upon graduation, the cash portion of this bequest will be turned over to him. In the meantime, he will continue to receive monthly payments from the trust."

Frankie interrupted to ask the lawyer to verify how much he'd be getting

"As I said, $12 million."

Eve was amazed at the amount. As for Frankie, he didn't like the condition on which the bequest rested, the financial studies. He had no mind for it and furthermore, as he told Eve later, no interest in it. However, his handsome inheritance would pay for the best tutor money could buy. His mind had already leapt ahead to figuring out a way for the tutor to impersonate him at exams.

"Now, as for you, madam, Mr. Overton bequeaths a cash payment of $15 million dollars in addition to assorted artwork and furnishings in his permanent suite at the Ritz Carlton Hotel in Montreal. Please note that his relationship with the hotel will be terminated shortly."

"That will be satisfactory," said the woman. Frankie stared at her. This was not the reaction he would have expected. Too calm and detached. As for Eve, she was shocked that Frankie's father could insult his only son that way. And how was Frankie staying so composed?

The lawyer then shuffled the papers on his desk into a neat pile.

"I believe that completes our business for today. Frankie, I'll get back to you about your father's suggestions for handling some of his assets. As he stood, so did the others. The mistress was the first to extend her hand. "Merci, monsieur." Eve followed, shaking the lawyer's hand. Frankie just said, "Bye, George."

At home, Frankie didn't mention the will at all. In fact, he didn't say much of anything. He seemed lost in thought. Since the reading of the will, Frankie was making her feel she wasn't even in the room. Finally, she went over to the phone and called Humph.

"So," Humph said, "how did Frankie make out in the will?"

"If you're not busy, I'd love to see you."

"I'm never busy now that the case appears to be closed. I'll get something for us to eat while you're on your way."

Earlier that morning, Duffy had dropped by to say the department was still refusing to let him make a second trip to Montreal.

"The case is closed, according to the chief of D's," Duffy said. "He said they had other cases for me to take over."

"Well from where I stand," said Humph, "the only thing unsolved is who killed Overton, and considering where it happened, that's a job for Montreal cops."

"I know, I know," said Duffy, "but I can't shake the feeling that there's more to the mistress connection than meets the eye. Like, why in the hell would she have come to New York to attend the la-di-da memorial of her sugar daddy. As far as I know, she doesn't know anyone here. Who would have even told her when and where the funeral was?"

Humph suggested Duffy write one of his French-Irish brothers on the Montreal force.

"Ask them if the case is really closed and whether they have any more thoughts about the mistress. You're stuck here anyway while you wait for an answer. Maybe your inquiry will stir things up and you'll get evidence that would justify you going back there."

"Do you always have such a clear head in the morning, Humph? A letter. That's a great idea."

Humph then admitted he felt the same itch as Duffy did but he no longer had a client involved in the case.

When Eve arrived, she immediately gave him the details of the will. What interested Humph the most beyond being happy for Eve's boyfriend was the presence of the mistress at the reading.

"It's a good thing the impetuous Detective Duffy didn't hop a train to Montreal right after the funeral," said Humph. "He was sure she was headed home. Actually, I would have thought so too."

They chatted of other things over lunch. When done, Eve motioned to Humph to sit still while she gathered the dishes and headed to the sink.

"Thank you," Humph said.

Over the clatter of dishes, he heard Eve's next question. Doing the dishes, he thought later, was Eve's way of not making the question too direct.

"So, Humph, what's with you and Karena?"

Had Eve still been a teenager, Humph would have called her a little rascal. He didn't mind talking about Karena but he had always thought matchmaking should be a crime.

"Out with it, Humph," Eve said as she turned off the water at the kitchen sink and hustled back to her chair at the table.

"Ever thought of becoming an interrogator for the NYPD?" Humph asked. He then got up and walked to the closet to get a jacket.

"Humph, it's a hot day if you hadn't noticed. I dare you to put on that jacket and keep it on for the next half hour."

Humph knew when he was beat.

"Actually, Eve..." He paused to take off the jacket, which he draped over the back of his chair.

"Actually?" Eve said.

"Actually, Eve, Karena and I are going to go on a little trip. Just a week. We both need to get out of the city."

"A cozy cabin in the Poconos?" Eve suggested.

"No. Florida."

When Eve said nothing, Humph added:

"For a week. Just a week."

Eve betrayed a little smile but remained silent.

"The idea is that, well Karena has never seen anywhere in the States except New York."

"So," said Eve, "this is just a geography lesson?"

"Who invited you here?" said Humph with clearly feigned annoyance.

He finally confessed that things were going well between him and Karena.

"Leave it at that, will you, Eve?"

The next day, Eve phoned back.

"About Florida…"

"Eve!" Humph interrupted as a warning.

"I talked to Frankie about your trip. He said September is the worst possible time to go to Florida. That's when they have hurricanes. Go in January instead, he said."

"Damn," Humph said. He admitted he didn't know a damn thing about the state. "That's one of the reasons I picked it. Suggestions?"

"The good old Poconos. Or even better, Niagara Falls," said Eve. "The honeymoon capital of the world."

"Goodbye, Eve."

"Wait, wait. One more thing. Frankie's article will be published two weeks from now."

CHAPTER 27

HUMPH found a copy of *True Manhattan Detective* at a newsstand on East Broadway and walked up to Seward Park to read it in the shade. It was already noon. Since his case was wrapped up, his working day habits had evaporated. Before going in search of the magazine, he stopped to chat with a knife sharpener on Cherry Street. Humph always wondered how he made a living going up and down the streets patiently pushing his little grinding table set on wheels. Humph was enjoying getting caught up with the many faces it seemed had always populated his neighborhood.

Getting comfortable on the park bench, Humph couldn't help but notice that Frankie's story appeared on the cover. The headline was "Booze, Dames and MURDER." The cover illustration portrayed a blonde gagged and bound and a small circular photo inset on the image showed a flotilla of trucks. Inserted on top of the small trucks was an illustration of a well-dressed gangster brandishing a Tommy gun.

Finally he found the story. It bore the byline Franklin Norwich. A nom de plume? Humph wondered. Or was Frankie intending on pocketing the inheritance then erasing his hated father from memory?

The story began accurately enough, recounting the injustice done to a naïve young rich man who wanted to impress his businessman father by scoring a great success on the stock market. The story described the shadow brokerages off Wall Street, the so-called and supposedly illegal bucket shops.

Frankie did a good job, thought Humph, of avoiding what must have been a strong temptation to dwell on the outrage of a father doing that to his son. The victim of the brokerage scam, however, had no knowledge at the time that his father was involved in his humiliation.

Next came the heinous kidnapping of a young dancer from her apartment on the Lower East Side, a devoted burlesque performer and occasional stripper who had never been in a speck of trouble her entire life. Upon hearing the news, a private detective who knew the young woman informed police that she had earlier revealed to him that the rich, big-shot broker frequented the strip club where she performed and had made it clear he wanted to take her under his wing. She was too street smart to fall for a line like that. Not long afterwards, the story said, the beautiful young woman was nowhere to be found, not at home, not on stage. Her many friends hadn't heard a peep from her in weeks.

"Despite investigative efforts by the police and the private detective, who betrayed a fatherly concern for her, no connection was found between the broker and the girl. However what investigators did discover was that the broker had business links with gangster Owney

Madden. As the layers of the onion were peeled back, it was determined that the broker and the gangster shared interests in trucking companies and speakeasies."

Here he quoted two police officers saying essentially the same thing, that there was often a futility in trying to discover who owned what when it came to organized crime.

It didn't take a genius, the story said, to link trucks, speakeasies and bootleg liquor.

Before police could get to the bottom of the relationship between the two, the broker was found murdered at his luxury abode at Gramercy Park. The killer has yet to be found.

The author listed some of the broker's millionaire clients. The magazine ran photos of several of them, giving the impression that they might have been involved in the broker's murder. Frankie wrote:

"All this reporter can say is that from that moment on, gangster Madden packed his bags and made his way to Arkansas, where the state's governor welcomed the evil Irishman and his goons, who were all put up in a luxury hotel. Police patrols were even assigned to make sure Madden wasn't disturbed."

More recently, the story said, it had been revealed that Madden not only left Arkansas but possibly left the country.

"The author can reliably report that there has been no sign of him in New York in months."

The story went on to say:

"Diligent work by undercover officers from the NYPD's Women's Division then provided the only success in this tangled web of greed and murder. The terrorized young dancer was rescued late one night from a speakeasy that doubled as a brothel. Both the gangster Madden and the dead broker owned speakeasies. The young woman was put in protective custody by the Women's Division officers.

"Our tale reached even more tragic proportions less than a month later when Randall Overton, the fabulously wealthy New York businessman and father of the young man duped of $10,000 by the now-dead broker, was himself murdered in cold blood. He was shot dead after dining at the swanky Ritz Hotel in Montreal. Police have no suspects.

"So far, police have been unable to make any connection between Overton's murder and New York investigations into bootlegging, kidnapping and murder, although it has been determined that he was a frequent visitor to Montreal and owned a major part of that city's largest distillery. He also owned extensive shipping interests.

"Dear reader, what you have read so far is an accurate account of this violent affair up to just days before publication. This reporter, long familiar with Montreal, travelled to the city to make inquiries with local police officers and conduct his own investigation.

"The following information is exclusive to *True Manhattan Detective*. New York police will read it at the same time you do.

"Randall Overton was murdered by his long-time mistress, Amélie St. Jean. I know that because I interviewed her. I already knew what she looked like because I spotted her at the funeral service for Overton in New York. I then heard from a private source that she came to attend the reading of Overton's will the next day. Then she disappeared.

"After getting to Montreal and talking with police, I learned that while Overton was shot to death in the hotel's posh restaurant, no weapon was ever found even though every diner had been questioned and searched. The mistress was there, too. As she often did, she had dined with Overton that day.

"On a hunch, I went to the hotel. I carried with me a note signed by the hotel manager granting me permission to question staff. Montreal police were no longer actively investigating the murder although the case was still open. I knew all guests that day had been questioned but there had been no mention of questioning restaurant staff. I took that upon myself. In my 12th interview, and despite language difficulties, I found a busboy who recalled emptying a champagne bucket much later on the evening of the murder and finding a small pistol immersed in the melted ice. It was surely placed there by the murderer. He said he never told police because he had to make sure he caught the last bus home and simply forgot about turning in the gun to his superiors. He agreed the pistol was small enough for a woman to easily handle it.

"I called police and was told the dead man's wound was caused by a small-caliber weapon.

"Instead of leaving the hotel, I learned the suite number for the late Mr. Overton. To my surprise and delight, the door was answered by the mistress. She said she was preparing to move out of the suite. It had been her home for years, even when Overton was not in town.

"Why would she confess to this reporter?"
"The simple answer is that I had the facts. The one lie I told was that the gun that killed Overton had been found by police. And, I told her, that I had learned that she was the closest person to him at the time of the shooting. The one thing the distraught coat-check girl remembered was seeing you right behind Overton. She said you were a familiar face because you dined so frequently with the dead man. In her account the night of the murder, she said she was so hysterical she may have forgotten to mention it to police.

"Amélie St. Jean listened without interrupting. When she spoke, her voice was calm, low and seductive.

"'Monsieur reporter,' she said. 'I have recently become one of the richest women in the city. As he did in life, Mr. Overton has treated me well in death. To be frank with you, I have more money than I can ever spend. Perhaps we can reach an arrangement, no?'"

"But, I asked, with my face just inches from hers,

'Why did you kill such a generous man?'

"Once again, her frankness stunned me."

"'Because I didn't want to wait for my money.'

"Your reporter, dear reader, of course said no to her offer. The woman didn't appear flustered. As I left the suite, she smiled and said, 'Think about it.'

"I didn't inform the local police about the confession and the gun because I wanted to return to New York and let you, my readers, be the first to know how this sordid case was solved."

Humph put down the magazine.

He thrust his fist in the air.

"Gotcha now!"

The park was almost deserted and only the squirrels stared at him. Humph rolled up the magazine and put it in his pocket.

"The best 25 cents I ever spent," he told the squirrels.

Humph had known something Frankie didn't. At Humph's advice, his pal Duffy had written Montreal police. They admitted they still didn't know who killed Overton in the restaurant but they at least were able to pass on a piece of new information. Overton's mistress was found stabbed to death in the suite at the Ritz. She'd been killed while packing a suitcase, which contained a considerable number of jewels as well as clothes. They had no suspect at the moment.

CHAPTER 28

THE first person Humph called that afternoon was Eve. He prayed that Frankie didn't answer.

The butler answered.

"Yes, sir. I'm afraid both parties are out. I don't know where young Mr. Overton is. However, I believe Miss Eve has gone to see a friend named Karena."

He phoned Karena.

"Eve tells me you wanted to take me to Florida in hurricane season."

"I've got some bad news for Eve. May I speak to her?"

"Yes, just give her a minute. She's trying on a new dress Frankie bought her."

When Eve got on the line, Humph wasted no time. He always thought that was the best way to deliver bad news.

"I have read Frankie's detective magazine story. It was good except for one thing, Eve. In trying to be clever, I'm afraid that he clearly incriminated himself by knowing about the gun and having visited the mistress at the hotel just before her death. I'm so sorry, Eve. I know you thought your relationship with Frankie was going somewhere."

There was no answer for more than a minute. Finally, Karena came on the line.

"Can she call you back? Whatever you told her hit hard. If she can't call I will, OK?"

It was Karena who called back.

"Tell me what you told her. She has shut herself in my bedroom."

Humph said Frankie had incriminated himself in the murder of his father's mistress, the woman they saw at the funeral.

"God, no!" said Karena. "The poor girl."

Here's the rest, said Humph.

"Frankie admitted in the story that he went to Montreal to continue the investigation into his father's death. I remember Eve telling me that Frankie was talking about going to Montreal to give shit to the distillery that let Frankie's father make him the signatory on orders that effectively were for bootleg whiskey destined to his father's warehouses in New York."

"It looks like he went for more than that," said Karena, who was more familiar with the investigation's details than Eve.

"No kidding," said Humph. "Before killing the mistress, Frankie proved through his own investigation that she had murdered his father. She said she did it because she didn't want to wait to get her hands on the inheritance. The thing is, Karena, Montreal police didn't know she murdered the old man. In his article, Frankie thought he was simply solving a crime. He confronted the mistress who tried to bribe him with money from the inheritance.

Had he accepted her offer, no one would ever have known she was a murderess. However, he decided to kill her. 'The only motive I can think of is that he wanted all the money. How much was it that the old man willed his mistress, $15 million? In writing a great story, he did himself in. It was one murder too many."

"Do our guys know?" Karena asked.

"Duffy's going to be my next call. I suspect he'll inform Montreal."

Duffy was delighted with Humph's detective work and the fact that he'd be the one to deliver the news to his new bosses.

"While they are singing my praises I'm going to ask if I could deliver the news to the Montreal cops in person."

"Incorrigible, Duffy. Be sure to buy a copy of the magazine to show your bosses. It's like a written confession."

Eve phoned mid-afternoon.

"Can I come over?"

"I was hoping you'd ask that. I wanted to see you in person."

Then, proving that she'd recovered a bit from the shock, Eve promised:

"I won't ask about you and Karena, or even suggest that things with you two are going somewhere."

Humph felt a hint tears in his eyes because Eve was herself again and back in his life the way she'd always been. He now enjoyed her teasing. Her mom would have approved. For some reason he remembered that the cobbler a block away on Henry Street was Ukrainian. Maybe he could teach him a few words of the language that would make Karena feel at home.

He phoned the train station.

"I know it's only September but can I reserve two return seats now to Miami for January?"

ABOUT THE AUTHOR

Wayne Clark is a Montreal writer and author of four
other novels, including the international award-winning
literary fiction novel he & She. In addition to writing fiction
he has worked as a journalist, copywriter and translator.

www.ingramcontent.com/pod-product-compliance
Lightning Source LLC
Chambersburg PA
CBHW071428260626
47170CB00008B/2636